NO ONE WRITES ROMANTIC FICTION
LIKE BARBARA CARTLAND.

Miss Cartland was originally inspired by the best
of the romantic novelists she read as a girl—
writers such as Elinor Glyn, Vere Lockwood and
E. M. Hull. Convinced that her own wide audi-
ence would also delight in her favorite authors,
Barbara Cartland has taken their classic tales of
romance and specially adapted them for today's
readers.

Bantam Books is proud to publish these novels—
personally selected and edited by Miss Cartland
—under the imprint

**BARBARA CARTLAND'S
LIBRARY OF LOVE**

Bantam Books by Barbara Cartland
Ask your bookseller for the books you have missed

Barbara Cartland's Library of Love series

Books of Love and Revelation

Other Books by Barbara Cartland

Son
of the
Turk

Vere Lockwood

Condensed by Barbara Cartland

SON OF THE TURK
A Bantam Book / June 1980

ISBN 0–553–13931–2

Published simultaneously in the United States and Canada

*Bantam Books are published by Bantam Books, Inc. Its trade-
mark, consisting of the words "Bantam Books" and the por-
trayal of a bantam, is Registered in U.S. Patent and Trademark
Office and in other countries. Marca Registrada. Bantam
Books, Inc., 666 Fifth Avenue, New York, New York 10019.*

PRINTED IN THE UNITED STATES OF AMERICA

0 9 8 7 6 5 4 3 2 1

Introduction

This dramatic, exciting story of the East was very popular at the time it was written. Young women dreamt of being abducted by dark-eyed, passionate Sheiks, Rajahs, and Beys, and I know you will enjoy the thrill of this exotic Eastern fantasy as much as I did.

—BARBARA CARTLAND

Chapter One
1929

The noise and bustle of Constantinople sent a murmur of conflicting sounds into a house in the European quarter.

Four men sat in the room talking.

"So, Colonel Wayne, you've come to get to the bottom of this matter? To find out what's happened to our representatives?" said General Gayham.

He was a wiry, sun-tanned man, and he addressed the man sitting opposite him, who was past the prime of life but was still upright and broad-shouldered in his neat drill suit.

"Yes, I've come to find out the truth, if it is possible."

"I hope you'll be successful," Captain Price, one of the men by the window, answered.

"It seems incredible," the Colonel went on, "that a certain man can be raising an anti-British feeling here and yet remain unknown. And what's more, the men we send to get information about him vanish without leaving any trace."

"If you know the Turks, Colonel," Captain Price said, "it won't seem so strange to you. They can be as close as oysters. Can't get a word we want from 'em."

"But, good Heavens," the Colonel said suddenly, "they daren't openly defy us! The authorities—"

"My dear Colonel, the matter's been before the authorities," General Gayham said. "You may be sure we shouldn't let a thing like this rest—"

"Well? What do they say?"

"Oh, they're all righteous indignation of course. Will find out what's happened to our people; will bring the offender to justice, and so forth, but—"

"Well?"

"The curse of the Turk, my dear Colonel— laziness. I don't think they want any unpleasantness with us, despite their desire to become independent, but nothing's done."

"I guessed it was pretty bad when I was sent here," the Colonel said, nodding.

"Bad enough that we're determined to clear up the matter." The General ground his glass upon the table. "We can't have any more trouble in the East. There's India, and we've only just got over Mesopotamia. We can't risk having trouble in Turkey.

"We've got to get this man. I'm very glad you've taken up this affair, Colonel Wayne. And I hope, with all my heart, that you'll be successful in the matter."

"What are your plans now, Colonel?" enquired the Captain from the window.

"I'm travelling into Turkey. Down to Aleppo and across to Bagdad. I'm going to try to find out who's encouraging lawlessness among the Turks and setting 'em against us. And I'm going to meet, in Bagdad, the Arab Chief, Suel el Sahab, to assure him of our goodwill."

The General's keen eyes met those of the Colonel.

"Our people were lost that way," said the former, evenly. "This person behind the mischief, a Turk no doubt, is trying to set the Arabs against us. Two envoys of ours journeyed to interview a certain powerful Arab. They were lost somewhere on the edge of the Syrian desert and have never been heard of since.

"Then Lieutenant Petersen arranged an interview with this same Suel el Sahab, but never kept it. He disappeared somewhere on the edge of the Syrian."

Colonel Wayne set his lips to a hard line. The more he heard of the affair the less he liked it.

"And you don't know who this person is? Have no suspicions of anyone?"

"No," Captain Price answered. "We only know that it's some pretty powerful Oriental."

"No, we suspect no-one," General Gayham went on. "Though I believe in Damascus they have suspicions of someone."

"It's little enough to go on," Wayne said. "But I mean to get to the bottom of this affair, to find the man."

"By Jove, I hope you do, Colonel," exclaimed Cameron. "And we'll give you all the assistance we can."

3

"Yes," the General said, "we'll be pleased to assist you."

"You don't travel alone, Colonel?" enquired Cameron.

"No. I have two of our people with me. Captain Hadley and Lieutenant Marsh. And between us we've a few men."

"I heard you'd come with a party, Colonel Wayne," broke in Cameron. "Captain Bray said you were travelling with your daughter."

"That is so." The elder man's grey eyes softened, his lips slightly relaxed. "I have my daughter, Daphnne, with me. She is travelling with some friends of ours, a Mr. and Mrs. Tennant, and their son and daughter."

"But is that wise, Colonel Wayne?" The General leant forward. "Having your daughter with you? It is hardly safe—"

The Colonel stopped him with a raised hand.

"You need not worry. I and my men are travelling with Daphnne and her party only as far as Aleppo. Then she and our friends will travel on to Damascus, sight-seeing, while I and my party go on our business to Bagdad."

"I see." The General sat back again, but a faint frown drew his brows together.

"And travelling in a party," continued Wayne, "will take away anyone's suspicions of my real business here."

"I'd like to meet your daughter," the General said, banishing his thoughts.

"We will be delighted to see you." Colonel Wayne looked at the watch on his wrist. "We're staying at the Feringee Hotel. And now, indeed, I must be going."

He rose to his feet, adding:

"It's very little information you can give me but I'll do my best to solve the whole problem."

*   *   *

Colonel Wayne stood on the terrace of the Feringee Hotel and watched a party of Europeans making their way up the road.

The party consisted of two girls and three men—Daphnne Wayne and Edith Tennant with their attendant cavaliers, Captain Hadley, Lieutenant Marsh, and Clive Tennant.

The Colonel's glance followed the figure of his daughter, a small, slim form in white coat and short skirt, and a soft, happy look was in his grey eyes.

As the party passed from his sight he turned from the balustrade and went back to a table on the terrace.

He reseated himself at the table and drew towards him two or three papers.

The noisy bustle of cosmopolitan life went on before the hotel. Yet Colonel Wayne appeared undisturbed by the noisy flow of life about him.

However, when an English voice addressed him, the Colonel looked up.

Captain Price had arrived in company with a tall, finely made Turk.

"What luck to find you alone, Sir." Captain and Colonel clasped hands. "Not that I shouldn't have liked to have seen your charming party. But this is a little visit of business. I want to introduce you to the Bey."

Captain Price glanced hastily over his shoulder, saw that the Turk with him had stopped to exchange a few words with an acquaintance at another table on the terrace, and bent swiftly towards the Colonel.

"He's the man who can help you with your work, Colonel. He's given us great assistance in our endeavours to solve this matter. He's heart and soul with us in wanting to catch the man who's playing the devil with us. And he's well up with the Turkish authorities so he's the very man to help us."

Taking leave of his acquaintance, the Turk came forward, a tall imposing figure upon the terrace.

The Colonel rose to his feet. Captain Price made the introduction.

"It is with extreme pleasure I make the *effendi* Wayne's acquaintance," said the Bey in almost perfect English.

Colonel Wayne looked at the man before him. The Bey was a fine figure, tall and broad-shouldered, fleshy more than muscular, perhaps, but the splendid form of a man, nonetheless.

A thorough Turk, possessing the hawk-like features, keen black eyes, and dark skin characteristic of his race.

Wayne could read little in the Turk's handsome face beyond the expression of pride and arrogance habitual to his race, and the dark eyes were baffling, inscrutable in their blackness.

"I'm pleased to meet you." The Colonel's voice was courteous. "It's good of you giving us your help, Bey."

A quick gesture of slim dark hands stopped him.

"It was but my duty."

Captain Price signalled a nearby waiter and the three men sat down at the table to drinks and cigarettes.

After a while, however, the Captain rose with a quick excuse and left the two men together.

"It is with great pleasure I learn the matter is being taken up," the Bey murmured.

"It's nice to know that someone in your position, Bey, is helping us."

"I am ready to help you to the most of my poor ability, *effendi*," returned Sueleman Bey. "It would not do for enmity to be again between my poor country and your great land."

Wayne nodded slowly.

"It would profit neither country. There's trouble enough out here as it is. But we must guard our own interests and people here—"

"Precisely. Your people, *effendi*, should be quite safe here. Since a certain person has broken the law regarding their safety—well, that person should be caught, made to suffer."

"You have no idea who the offender is?"

The Turk's fine shoulders went up.

"I am desolated. I know, *effendi*, that it is someone rich and powerful who offends. Someone who has authority. But what are your plans, *effendi*? That is," he went on quickly, "if one so unworthy as myself may enquire."

"Of course!" exclaimed Colonel Wayne genially. "I have to interview Suel el Sahab, the Chief poor Petersen failed to meet—"

"Ah!" A faint gleam showed for a moment in the Turk's black eyes.

"Oh, I don't intend to be taken like our other

people," the Colonel laughed shortly. "I know a bit about the East."

"But yes." The Bey's voice was a soft murmur. "It would be just deplorable if harm came to you, *effendi*. Where do you meet Suel el Sahab? Do you travel down to Arabia?"

"No, I have to meet the Chief in Bagdad."

"Ah."

"And, moreover, I have to clear up the matter of our people's disappearance."

"You travel to Bagdad, and then to the Syrian, *effendi*?" enquired the Bey courteously.

"No; I travel to Aleppo and then to Bagdad and back to the Syrian," answered the Colonel.

"You do not travel alone, *effendi*?" murmured the Turk. "You have, of course, some of your own people with you?"

"Oh yes, but we're quite a small party."

"Ah." The faint gleam in the Turk's eyes softened the rather hard expression on his dark face.

"Will you not accept some assistance from me, *effendi*? Will you not accept some of my men, to accompany you—?"

"No, no, Bey; we're in your debt already. But you see, we're travelling as a tourist-party. To take a number of men with us wouldn't be diplomatic."

"Ah." The Bey's dark eyes glinted beneath their heavy lashes. "I see. Precisely. But—even as you travel," he murmured. "I fear you will have a very difficult task."

* * *

On a fair, warm morning two days after his first meeting with Ahmad Sueleman Bey, Colonel

Wayne sat on the hotel terrace talking with a man from the Embassy.

At a table next to his sat his daughter, Daphnne, and Lieutenant Marsh, a member of his party.

Her features were small and delicate, her eyes were large and of a slightly darker grey than her father's, and her hair fair, short and curly, was a natural golden crown for her fair-skinned face.

Daphnne looked often but a child with her short curls and small form, but the round curves of a lovely figure dispelled the illusion.

At this moment another of the Colonel's party, Captain Hadley, a tall, fair-haired Englishman, stepped onto the terrace.

He passed Wayne and the other man with a quick word of greeting and, taking from under his arm half-a-dozen illustrated magazines, placed them on the table before the fair girl.

"There, Miss Wayne, I've raked up that amount. And you'll find one or two, at least, quite up-to-date! Compliment me, for you know I deserve it!"

She looked up, laughing.

"Oh, men and your rewards!"

"Oh, women with your denials!" the Lieutenant retaliated.

Colonel Wayne's light brows were slowly knitting over his grey eyes.

He was endeavouring to keep his thoughts upon his own conversation, but the light, bantering chatter at the other table made it difficult for him to do so.

Two more young people came onto the terrace—a tall, dark girl and her dark, more effeminate brother—Edith and Clive Tennant of the party.

The quick, light conversation increased. Colonel Wayne gave up all thought of continuing his own thoughts and discussion.

With the man from the Embassy he turned and joined his daughter's party.

Colonel Wayne had one great weakness—his daughter. A widower with one child, he lavished upon this one daughter all the affection of his kind, genial nature.

Hard though he could sometimes be, there was nothing that he could refuse this slim, lovely, golden-haired daughter of his.

Daphnne sat back in her chair. The others went on to talk of the shops and bazaars, and she slipped out of the conversation. Looking over the balustrade, she regarded the street.

The East attracted and yet repelled her. Alluring, mysterious, picturesque, it held her so that she could not resist its attraction. It stirred a strange longing in her heart.

Yet, at other times, it aroused a faint but nonetheless real fear in her—a fear of its mystery, its sinister, veiled obscurity.

"The General's giving us a visit this evening." The Lieutenant's voice speaking softly beside her half-startled her. "I'm afraid we'll never let you go from us, Miss Wayne."

The caressing glance of his dark eyes resting on her said far more than his words.

"You'll have to," she said, dismissing her thoughts with a light laugh. "I want to go farther into the country, see something that's older, more Eastern—"

She looked along the terrace. A tall Turk was ascending the steps to the hotel entrance.

She glanced at him idly at first and then with more interest. She thought she had never seen a finer figure of a man.

"We'll keep you here as long as we can, Miss Wayne," Captain Hadley was saying. "I say you're our golden luck."

"How nice of you. But really, I hope I may be," she said, smiling at the fair man. "It's a pity you've got to go off on that horrid business and our party's to be broken up—"

She stopepd short. The tall Turk she had seen enter the hotel appeared upon the terrace and walked up to their table. She saw her father rise and greet him and then present him to their party.

With a perfect courtesy Sueleman Bey acknowledged the introductions, slightly bowing to each, giving each a quick, keen glance from beneath his heavy black lashes.

Ahmad Sueleman Bey. Daphnne knew him then, for her father had spoken to her of him.

The Bey had straightened from bowing to Edith Tennant and looked across at her.

As the Turk's glance rested on the fair white girl, his tall, upright figure seemed to stiffen, and his narrowed eyes opened, a bright, intense gleam in their depth.

Indeed, Daphnne was a fair, lovely picture reclining in her chair; small figure light-clothed, fair skin as yet untouched by the Eastern sun, eyes grey and shadowed, hair short and a gleaming, arresting mass of drawn-back curls.

Faint colour slightly warmed Daphnne's cheeks. She was used to the ardent, admiring looks of men, but the Turk's regard was such to which she could not remain indifferent.

Even the others at the table seemed aware of the Turk's fixed look, and after a moment Sueleman Bey struggled to command himself.

For the first time in his life he had been taken off his guard, had been stirred by the sudden, lovely picture of this fair English girl.

For a moment he was disconcerted, then, the next, had regained his habitual perfect control of himself. He moved round the table.

"*Mademoiselle*, this is the happiest day of my life—this on which I make *Mademoiselle*'s acquaintance."

Daphnne murmured some conventional words of greeting and, unused to Eastern customs, held out her hand.

The Bey, without the least hesitation, took her fingers with his and bent over them. His lips did not touch her hand but Daphnne experienced a strange feeling as he held her fingers, felt a thrill, whether of excitement or fear she could not tell.

His dark, heavy-lashed eyes looking into hers as he raised his head held her—slightly attracted her.

He released her hand and sank with lithe grace into the chair an attentive waiter brought forward.

The Bey seemed thoroughly educated, could speak well upon almost every matter. He talked politics with the men yet would turn to the girls and discuss his country and various sights of interest there.

As the Bey rose to take his leave, he said a few quick words to Daphnne.

"*Mademoiselle*, you are travelling through Turkey, my poor country?"

"I am travelling down to Damascus, Bey. We wish to see a little of the East."

"*Mademoiselle*, it would give me great pleasure to show you some little of it, some few of the places of interest."

"It is most kind of you, Bey." Daphnne's darkened lashes veiled her eyes from the intense glance of his.

He was a splendid, imposing figure to regard, but the flame which showered in the black eyes disturbed her.

"You are already helping my father. I could not think of giving you any more trouble."

"Trouble, *Mademoiselle!* It would be a most exquisite pleasure."

Then, with his quick courtesy, he turned and addressed the others and, a few minutes later, took leave of the European party.

* * *

Captain Price, standing on the steps of the Feringee Hotel, crushed in his hand the message he had received.

A little above him on the terrace stood Daphnne Wayne and Edith and Clive Tennant.

It was the last day of the Europeans' stay in

Constantinople. The previous day they had heard of a certain mosque they had not visited.

Daphnne wanted to see it at once but the others had not been so enthusiastic.

However, Captain Price, ever ready to please the English girl, had planned to take the party that day. As they were about to start, the message had been brought to him.

When he had first deciphered the message a wild excitement had gripped Captain Price.

But after a while that excitement slowly left him. They had had so many disappointments. This wonderful chance surely could not mean anything. Conquest surely could not be right.

Captain Price smoothed out the crumpled letter and studied the message again.

> *I think we have the man we want. He is interviewing an Egyptian, Muri Saladin, to-morrow, Wednesday morning at the Akserai Café in Mushput.*
>
> *Start at once for Mushput with some re-liable men. See Abdul Seri at the café, he will help you. This time I know the information is correct. We have the man, if you can get to Mushput in time. Best wishes for success.*
> *Julian Conquest*

Coming to the signature, the Captain pictured the writer of the message—the slim dark young man who, by determination and hard work, had forced his way up to be Lieutenant Conquest. He was quartered in Damascus and was working upon this matter of finding the man responsible for all the trouble.

14

Yet it hardly seemed possible that after all their failures and difficulties they were to succeed so soon.

But if he, the man, was to be in Mushput at a certain café at a certain time—they had him!

"Bad news, old bean?" Clive Tennant's rather effeminate voice hailed him from the terrace.

The Captain started, becoming aware of his surroundings. He frowned slightly, thinking of the trip that had been planned for that morning and that he would have to disappoint the Colonel's fair, lovely daughter.

He crushed the note in his hand with faint anger. But it could not be helped.

Turning, he sprang up the steps to the terrace.

"I'm most awfully sorry. I hate to disappoint you. But I'm afraid I shan't be able to take you to see the mosque now—"

"Oh!" Daphnne's faint exclamation was full of disappointment, as the Captain had feared.

"I'm so sorry," he hurried on. "It's a beastly disappointment for me too."

"But why—?"

"I've got to go to Mushput," explained the Captain.

"But must you go at once?"

"I'm afraid so."

"Oh, have a heart, old man," chimed in Clive. "How can I look after 'em?" He waved a nonchalant hand towards the two girls. "They're so dashed determined to go. And I don't understand the bally customs and language."

"It's unfortunate," said Edith. "But of course we mustn't keep you, Captain Price."

Daphnne swung her short, scarlet sunshade and stared down at the street. She wanted to go to the mosque!

"I'm awfully sorry," exclaimed the Captain again.

"And the Bey's not here this morning to take us," she murmured.

Captain Price stiffened slightly, frowned. Lately, Ahmad Sueleman Bey had been a constant visitor at the Feringee Hotel.

The Turk had entertained the Europeans at his fine house in the residential quarter and had arranged trips for them with a skill that revealed his influential position.

The Captain did not like the Bey's growing intimacy with the Waynes and the Tennants.

Daphnne, having noticed the man's expression from beneath her lashes, looked suddenly up at him.

"Can't you really come with us, Captain Price?"

The man flushed beneath his tan and moved uncomfortably.

"I'm afraid I can't, Miss Wayne. I can't say how it hurts me to disappoint you. But I have to go—"

She moved up to him and laid one small white hand on his arm.

"Can't you come with us to the mosque first, Captain Price, and then catch the train to this place where you've got to go?"

The man looked down into the soft grey eyes raised to his.

Duty called him one way, but the soft, lovely eyes lured him the other. He was acutely conscious of her lissom body, so near to him. Her slim fingers on his arm had greater strength to move him than the note he had crushed in his pocket.

"Won't you take me to the mosque first?" she murmured.

"By Jove, I wonder if I could. One moment; I'll just see if I can—enquire about the trains." He turned and hurried into the hotel.

Daphnne lifted her sunshade and laughed softly.

In a few minutes the Captain was back on the terrace.

"Yes, I can just do it!" he exclaimed. "There's only one train to Mushput but it doesn't start for an hour or so. Come along, we'll just have time to have a look at the mosque."

The mosque was found, inspected, and discussed. The swiftly flying minutes became hours.

Captain Price had to hurry to his lodgings and swiftly pack a bag, had a greater hurry and bother to collect the men he wanted, and then rushed with them to the terminus.

When they reached the station, however, it was to learn that the only train to Mushput had gone.

Chapter Two

Nismin, about a hundred miles from Trenedad, was a small town with a very cosmopolitan
populace.

On the balcony of the small hotel, Colonel
Wayne was seated with his fair-haired daughter.
The party of Europeans, on their journey to Aleppo, had taken almost all the rooms the small hotel
could boast of.

The Colonel sat at a small table, studying papers and writing.

Daphnne sat in an easy-chair, a few magazines on the floor beside her. The balcony ran
the length of the hotel, with half-a-dozen steps
leading down to the street from the centre.

The girl stretched her small, rounded limbs
in the canvas chair. It was a warm summer afternoon.

The spell of the East was still on Daphnne;
the wonder of the bazaars, the beauty of strange
houses.

The fatigue and worry of travelling had not
lessened the attraction of the country for her,
though at times they had journeyed with great
discomfort.

The Colonel threw aside two letters.

"Well, that's done. Didn't the Bey say he was coming to Nismin, Daf?"

"I believe he did say something about coming here. Isn't it strange he was travelling down the same way we were, right from Constantinople!"

"Very convenient, Daf," said the Colonel. "Thoroughly decent chap. He's helped us pretty well. We'd never have travelled as comfortably and quickly as we have if it hadn't been for him."

"Yes, he's certainly been very good," murmured Daphnne, and thought of the big Turk who had the power to attract her—who looked at her with the gleam of fire in the depths of his dark eyes.

"Do you know, Father, he was telling me about his palace, where he's going now. I should think it must be lovely. He wanted us to visit it. I wish we could go, if only for a few days, just to see it."

Wayne shook his head.

"Can't be done, Daf. I've got to travel on to Bagdad. We can't fail Suel el Sahab again."

"It seems so strange that you can't clear up this affair." Daphnne knitted arched brows in a frown. "Do you really think they killed our people?"

"Our men have never been heard of since," said the Colonel grimly. "But don't worry your pretty head over the matter, child."

Daphnne did not.

"Don't you think the Bey will help you, Father?"

"I do," said Wayne. "I've faith in him. I think he'll help us more than anyone else."

A small motor-car rattled down the street and came to a noisy stop before the little hotel. A young man in Turkish dress got out.

Daphnne, leaning forward, regarded him.

He turned to the native driver of the car, spoke to him in a foreign tongue, turned again, and pushed his way through the cosmopolitan passers-by to the balcony steps.

He appeared quite unconscious of the watching regard of a woman's interested, calculating eyes. He had the appearance of a young *effendi* of good family. Daphnne had seen many like him since her arrival in Turkey.

Yet—Daphnne was forced to admit to herself—there was some strange difference about this one which she could not quite place.

Even as he had pushed through the crowd on the path there had seemed something different about him from the other Turks. Perhaps it was his clean, neat dress, his lithe movements, or his slim, straight figure which seemed to speak of a perfect physical condition.

On the balcony he stopped and looked at the various rooms. It seemed then that he felt the regard of the girl, for, turning slightly, he looked at her.

Daphnne caught her breath, felt her heart leap suddenly. She was stirred as never her first meeting with Ahmad Sueleman Bey had stirred her, held in the grip of a strange excitement that she could not understand.

Never, she thought, had she seen more lovely golden eyes; eyes that stared steadily at her and then brightened with a faint gleam.

She found herself unable to look away, held

in a spell that made the noisy world about her become vague, of little importance.

To the man, the picture of the fair English girl upon the balcony was one that would remain ever in his memory. She sat in her chair, bending slightly forward, her hands clasped about her knees, her silk-clad legs crossed before her.

A small, lovely face he saw, short gold curls stirred by the faint wind, and eyes very dark and wide.

To him she was the most lovely girl he had ever seen, and he had seen lovely women of many countries.

A strain of Latin in his nature gave him an ardent temperament, a quick temper, but he had put all his virile young manhood into work, hard, skilful.

Temptations had come his way but he had resisted them, and, looking at the fair, lovely little English girl, he thought he could understand why he had successfully passed by those temptations.

His wide golden eyes acknowledged her beauty, her feminine attraction.

Still looking at her, the man slightly smiled, showing white teeth against a dark skin—a skin faintly darker than the hue of deep tan.

Daphnne drew her breath quickly. With her pulses throbbing a little, her glance held by his, she strove to escape from the spell of his look— to keep from smiling back.

"Ha. Thinking of tea, Daf?" The Colonel put the last paper he had studied on the pile before him.

It was not so commonplace a thing as tea

that was troubling Daphnne, however, but something far more strange and wonderful—something she could hardly understand.

The young man was forced at last to drag his look from the girl, to turn and address one of the hotel-attendants.

After a moment the native pointed to Wayne's table, and Daphnne saw the man's face change, become hard, cold, his eyes darken.

Curtly he dismissed the native and came along the balcony.

"Pardon me. You are Colonel Wayne?"

The Colonel looked up sharply and saw a young man in neat Turkish dress standing a pace from the table.

"Yes, I'm Colonel Wayne."

Again Daphnne saw the younger man's face harden. There was a pause and then he seemed to force himself to speak.

"I thought that perhaps I might find you here. I wish to see Captain Price. Is he travelling with you?"

"Captain Price?" the Colonel questioned. "No, he's not with us. He's in Constantinople. But—"

"I am Julian Conquest," explained the young man briefly.

"Ah." The Colonel looked with greater interest at the man before him. So this was Julian Conquest.

It was something of a surprise to the Colonel to find him a man so young, and yet, looking at the hard set of the face and the almost arrogant carriage of the dark head, Wayne knew him to be a man to accomplish things.

"Lieutenant Conquest? I'm most pleased to meet you. This is my daughter, Daphnne."

The younger man clasped the Colonel's hand for but a moment; he scarcely glanced at the girl, who murmured something unintelligible.

"Won't you sit down—?"

"I'm sorry, but I have a very short time to spare." There was no softening in the young man's tone.

Daphnne, sitting back in her chair, was able to regard the man from beneath her lashes.

She admitted to herself that it was an exceedingly good-looking face; the regular features, the dark skin, and the hazel eyes with their dark lashes made it extremely attractive.

A red tarboosh with a blue, swinging tassel was on his head, giving him a look of height, and he wore a long, light Turkish coat over riding-breeches and light shoes.

"I wish to see Captain Price," he went on, "I thought perhaps he was travelling with you—?"

"No, no," the Colonel broke in. "He's quartered at Constantinople, you know. But was it about that affair of your message you wished to see him?"

"Yes." The word was short and brief; then: "You know, then, about it?"

"Yes," admitted the Colonel. "He told me and showed me your message. I was very sorry—"

"Then perhaps you can tell me why Captain Price didn't go to Mushput, didn't act upon that message?" The younger man's voice was hard and cold.

Colonel Wayne stiffened slightly in his chair. He felt a sense of hostility in the other's attitude.

"He lost the train."

"Indeed?" The level brows rose above the hazel eyes. "Didn't my message reach him in time?"

"Yes, he got your message all right, I think, but—"

"Then why was it he missed the train?"

Colonel Wayne flushed slightly. He sensed in the young man before him a figure of censure and resentment.

The Colonel had never been addressed in such a way before, and his own voice hardened.

"It was an unfortunate accident. Captain Price had planned that morning to take my daughter and some friends to see a mosque, and when he got to the station the train was gone. It was unfortunate. I was very sorry—"

The younger man drew back slightly, his hands clenching suddenly at his sides. He hardly credited what he heard.

He had been so sure of Captain Price. Now, when so much, everything, in fact, rested upon him—he had failed them.

He turned slightly, looked at the fair English girl who had set so strange a spell upon him at first sight, and thought he could understand why the Captain had failed him.

The spell of her beauty gripped him—held him again. The blue-greyness of half-closed eyes ... the whiteness of fair skin ... the sweet curves of lissom body ...

Through his anger and bitterness he was conscious of another powerful, surging emotion—of the warm blood in his face.

Angrily he mastered himself—struggled free

24

of the allure of her loveliness—her feminine attraction.

Yes, he could understand why Captain Price had failed them.

Anger surged in him; the rage which suddenly showed in his eyes made them gleam like pure gold.

Daphnne drew a quick breath, felt her heart racing at unusual speed. He seemed positively furious.

But she did not feel very much afraid, though never before had anyone looked at her with such anger.

She was also a little angry. His utter disregard of her, his hard, imperative demeanour, aroused in her a feeling of rebellion that she had never experienced before.

He stiffened a little. As he had looked at her on the balcony she had seemed everything that was sweet and lovely and desirable. But the loveliness of hers covered a shallow, pleasure-loving soul—a selfish heart.

Yes, he could judge her quite well. The influential Colonel's daughter, petted, pampered, spoilt! A lovely doll, playing with the lives of men.

His thoughts were angry and bitter. He smiled cynically and his look made the girl suddenly furious.

"No-one is to blame. It was a most unfortunate accident. Was it very important—?"

"It was the sort of accident that costs men their lives, Colonel Wayne."

"What do you mean?"

"As long as this Turk is at liberty, the lives of

our men are in danger," the hard, young voice returned.

"Do you mean that we had a chance of getting the man at Mushput?"

"It was a chance that I think we shan't get again. We could not have reached Mushput in time, but I had faith in Captain Price."

Colonel Wayne's hand clenched slowly on the table. Only now was he aware of the chance that had slipped by them, for Captain Price had been somewhat vague in his explanation.

"Believe me, Lieutenant Conquest, I'm exceedingly sorry about this. I understand now the chance we have let go."

The Colonel's voice was sincere and the younger man's attitude softened a little, for, despite himself, he felt drawn towards this grave, keen, soldierly man.

His feelings with regard to the fair girl, however, did not change.

"Won't you sit down?" Wayne spoke quickly, for the other had moved back as if to depart.

"I'm sorry, I can't," returned the other coldly. "At the moment I'm very busy. But if at any time I can give you assistance, Colonel Wayne, I shall be pleased to do so if my work allows.

"At the moment I'm staying at the Orient Palace in Trenedad. I'm known there by the name of Dara Samara. I wish you every success, Colonel Wayne."

He gave a slight bow to the elder man, cast a narrowed, half-mocking glance at the girl, and, turning, strode lithely along the balcony.

Daphnne clenched her hands on the magazine

she had picked up, on a pretence of reading, with almost childish rage.

Never before had a man spoken to her father and so utterly ignored her! Never before in all her successful life had she been treated with such indifference! It was as if she had not existed. Never before had she experienced such a thing!

Daphnne was furious; furious as she had never been before in all her life.

"Gad!" exclaimed the Colonel as the slim figure in Turkish dress swung down the steps and entered the small waiting car. "What a strange fellow!"

"My dear father, surely you can see what he is. He's a Turk."

"What!"

"Father dear, look at his dress, his dark face, his ways. You can see at once he's a Turk."

"But—he's Lieutenant Conquest—"

"So he says." Her voice was mocking. "Surely you're not deceived by that. He's a Turk, Father."

Gathering up her magazines, she rose and walked stiffly from the balcony into her room.

* * *

Daphnne wondered if she would ever again see that slim, cool young man who, in his visit to her father, had burst so suddenly in upon her pleasant tranquillity.

However, it was only the day following his coming to the hotel that she met him for the second time.

She was strolling in a little public garden with

Lieutenant Marsh when she saw the man who had taken such unauthorised possession of her thoughts walking along a path a little below their own.

"What is it, Miss Wayne?" The young Lieutenant was immediately aware of his fair companion's straying attention.

Daphnne nodded a neat head towards the nonchalant figure strolling a little below them.

"Who's that man?"

The Lieutenant looked down to view the enemy—and was not very reassured on recognising that individual.

"Why—that's Lieutenant Conquest."

"So you also think he's Lieutenant Conquest?" she said.

"Why, yes," exclaimed the young man. "Captain Hadley and I met him last evening."

"I don't believe he's Lieutenant Conquest at all," she said.

"Gad—"

"Now, does he look an Englishman?"

Marsh looked down at the good-looking face, so dark of skin, so regular of feature, the almost arrogant carriage of the lithe figure—and was forced to admit the truth.

"No; but I suppose he has to dress like that, you know. He'd never learn anything if he worked for us as a European."

"Look at his dark face," she went on.

"Well, I expect he's got pretty tanned working in this infernal climate."

"No, he's darker than that. Why, you're a dark Englishman and you're well tanned, but you're quite light compared to him."

"Say, do I take that as a compliment? But honestly, do you mean to say you think he's a Turk?"

"I do. Let's go back and down the steps. We'll catch him at the bottom then."

So it was that Julian Conquest looked up to see a slim, fair girl on the arm of a tall young Englishman confronting him.

They stood almost in his path. Daphnne saw the quick gleam of his hazel eyes as he looked at her.

His dress was now less correct; the long coat was open, showing a light shirt beneath. She thought he looked more careless, less Oriental in appearance.

Marsh quickly broke the silence, greeting the other man and introducing the girl at his side.

"Oh, yes, we've met before," Daphnne said in her most nonchalant tone. "'You called on my father yesterday, I believe?"

Julian Conquest smiled slightly.

"As you are perfectly aware, Miss Wayne."

Daphnne flushed and gripped her sunshade.

Marsh took up the conversation, pleased with what he had to say, for in all other males he saw possible rivals.

"D'you know, Conquest, Miss Wayne thought you were a Turk. That comes of dressing up in those things, you see."

The golden eyes gleamed for a moment, and then were slightly narrowed.

"Oh, I can quite understand Miss Wayne would think something like that," returned the other with the utmost coolness. "Miss Wayne has

29

seen so very little of life—out here—that she cannot very well judge."

Daphnne almost gasped. He was angry, she knew, but he controlled himself so well—answered back in a way that made her the more angry.

Certainly he was a type of man she had never met before. Never before had a man known her and not paid homage to her beauty—her feminine charm.

She wondered how those golden eyes would look when they were tender . . . what the touch of those slender, tanned fingers would be like. . . .

With suddenly warm cheeks she dismissed her thoughts. She couldn't even attempt to attract him since he made her so angry.

"I say—" began Marsh, but Daphnne cut in:

"My bag! Oh, I must have dropped it up on the other path."

Lieutenant Marsh, after a slight hesitation, sprang up the steps to the other path.

"I daresay, Miss Wayne," coolly went on the other man, "I can be sufficiently Turkish for your liking."

"Oh, you're that already," swiftly returned the girl.

He laughed slightly and stood back, regarding her.

She was a fair enough picture, attired in a short, white, clinging dress with a red belt and hat and a small sunshade across one shoulder.

Very English—gloriously sweet and fresh she looked in that hot, dusty, Eastern garden.

Little could she know of the East. Blindly she came into it with her loveliness imperiling and not protecting. . . .

Knowing that land, he wondered what her fate would be.

But before she was caught by inevitable Fate, how many men would have to suffer through her selfishness, her wilfulness—

"It's a great surprise to see you here," she went on. "I thought you were so awfully busy. I thought you really hadn't a moment to spare."

He knew that she was mocking him and his Latin temper was quickly aroused. His hazel eyes glinted between their darker lashes.

He had a sudden overmastering desire to touch her ... grip her ... crush her slim little body against his ... silence with his own her small, mocking lips. ...

He knew—and the knowledge was strangely sweet—that, held in his arms, she would not be so cool and mocking.

She had always done as she pleased, had always had her own way. She had never known the will—or the strength—of another greater than her own.

It would be sweet to make her feel a mastery which now she did not guess could be.

To hold her perfect little form helpless in his arms ... to feel her lips under his ...

Such thoughts brought the warm blood to his face. He felt the throb of quickened pulses ... the sudden surge of primitive feelings ... of virile desires within him.

Angrily he mastered himself.

"Do you often come here?" she enquired, striving to be utterly indifferent to his look. "I thought yesterday you were finding life so awfully trying."

"Oh, no," he returned. "I find life very interesting; more interesting than you've known it to be."

"Why?"

"Because you've never known it at all," he said.

"Really?"

"Your world does not let you," he went on. "It's an artificial world to which you belong, and it does not let you know what real life can be—"

He broke off as Lieutenant Marsh sprang down the steps with the lost bag.

She thanked Marsh with unusual warmth and slipped her free hand beneath his arm.

"I do hope you won't have any more unpleasant accidents to hinder you with your work, Lieutenant Conquest," she said as they departed.

"Thank you, Miss Wayne, but I rarely have such accidents," swiftly returned Conquest, and, turning, he continued his leisurely stroll along the path.

Chapter Three

Daphnne Wayne, looking through an opalescent haze of smoke from cigarettes and burning incense, gazed at the long, wide room of the Café Orient.

On one side of her sat Captain Hadley, on the other Lieutenant Stuart, a young subaltern from the Consulate in Trenedad.

Their table was at the extreme end of the room, opposite the big, arched entrance. She could get but a vague impression of the room at first.

The atmosphere was close, sensuous. After the coolness of the street from which they had come, the air came about her like a hot, scented cloak— stifling, overpowering. . . .

The Café Orient had a reputation which was not exactly the most blameless.

There had been more than one disturbance within it and about its vicinity, though nothing very serious had been brought up against its proprietors.

It was while the party of Waynes and Tennants were staying in Trenedad that the café was heard of.

The only member of the party who showed any great desire to visit the place was the Colonel's daughter, and she, having her own way in the matter as usual, was escorted to the café by Captain Hadley and Lieutenant Stuart.

"I don't for a moment think they'd try any tricks on us," Lieutenant Stuart remarked.

"Hope you're right. All the same, I wish you hadn't come here, Daf—Miss Wayne."

"Oh, but, Captain Hadley, I just had to have a look at the place. I had to see a real Eastern café. I want to get into the true atmosphere."

"Lord, you've got the atmosphere here all right, Miss Wayne!" Stuart waved his hand above their table to move a cloud of smoke. "Phew!"

Daphnne, laughing a little, looked again down the café room. It was a scene full of interest to the white girl. Attractive—sinister perhaps.

The faces of the men, indolent, indifferent, arrogant or cruel, vicious or cunning, all showed different types. Daphnne felt as if she had stepped from the outside world into a part of the mysterious, sensuous, surging East.

The droning music was monotonous ... yet palpitating. The heavy, smoke-laden, hashish-scented air enveloped her. . . . She strove to throw off the spell which was slowly stealing over her— to resist the almost sinister, luring attraction of the place.

The native players struck up another tune, and from behind a curtain at their side of the room a slim, dark girl in velvet jacket and long green trousers came forward and danced in the clear space on the floor.

The Turks appeared to regard every movement of the dance with attention but the Englishmen were less interested.

"You're not entranced, Lieutenant?"

"Lord, Miss Wayne, give me credit for liking something more graceful and pretty!" cried the young subaltern; then, bending to her: "Y'know— I'm entranced—elsewhere!"

"You don't think— Why, what is it, Daf?"

Daphnne's hand had suddenly gripped Captain Hadley's arm with a strength that made him break off and turn quickly towards her.

She was looking down the café room.

A young Turk had entered the café—a slim, dark man who walked with a leisurely, graceful stride between the tables and couches up the room.

"Well, I'm hanged!" cried Lieutenant Stuart.

"Conquest—here! I thought—" added the Captain, his fair brows puckering in a frown.

Stuart made a movement in his chair but the girl's white hand came now suddenly on his arm.

"Don't take any notice of him! He doesn't seem to have seen us. Look, the girl's ending her dance."

Nonchalantly, the dark young man walked up the room, acknowledging the greeting of a native here and there.

Covertly the white girl regarded him. He was in complete Turkish dress. He wore long, full green trousers tightened in at the ankle, a small jacket over a thin shirt, slippers with curled toes, and a scarlet cap.

The native dress revealed to advantage his slim, supple figure. He looked the perfect arrogant young Turk.

Halfway up the room he met another young Turk, and the two stood talking. Daphnne caught her breath. They were so much alike that she had a sudden stab of painful feeling.

For some minutes they stood together talking and then he of the paler skin moved forward and strolled to a couch at no great distance from the table at which the Europeans sat.

He took no notice of the English people. The dark lashes veiled the regard of his eyes. An attendant swiftly approached him with coffee.

"You want to convince me that man's an Englishman! He's pretty familiar with the natives here."

"But—"

A native attendant approached them with fresh cups of coffee.

Half-a-dozen more Turks entered the café and seated themselves on chairs near the three English people. The golden eyes of the man on the couch by himself noted their arrival.

"I can't understand it." The young subaltern pushed aside his coffee cup. "The man's known to us as Lieutenant Conquest."

"But, Gad, to look at him, one wouldn't question his being a Turk!" exclaimed the Captain. "D'you know Conquest here?"

"Yes, the General knows him." Stuart spoke of their head at the British Consulate in Trenedad. "And he's accepted this man."

"Can't make it out," exclaimed Hadley. "Even in native dress an Englishman'd look a bit different here. But this chap's the Turk to the life."

Daphnne laughed—short, cool laughter.

"Surely it's not so hard to understand. The

man's a Turk, all right. He says he's taking the name of Dara something, but that's his real name. He's a Turk masquerading as this Lieutenant Conquest."

"Gad!"

"You know Father said you're up against a pretty cunning lot in these natives. I expect this young Turk's the spy of that man you want to get. He's calling himself Lieutenant Conquest to get among you."

"Good Heavens; if that should be so!" exclaimed the young subaltern.

"You see," went on the girl, "he's taken no notice of us here."

It seemed to give Daphnne infinite pleasure to run down the man who sat at no great distance from them.

His slim, supple figure reclining indolently on the couch made her angry; his lazy attitude and cool nonchalance annoyed her.

In all that room full of Orientals she was conscious most of his presence. And although he had not once looked up or noticed them, she felt he was aware of her as she was aware of him.

"Say, Daf, haven't you had about enough of this? I think we'd better be going—"

Captain Hadley did not finish, for, even as he was speaking, the café door at the other end of the room shut with a sudden clang and immediately the Turks rose as one man and flung themselves towards the Europeans' table.

The white girl, with a faint cry, sprang up and staggered back against the wall behind their table.

For just a moment, and for the first time in her

easy life, she experienced fear as she saw the dark faces of the crowd of men who sprang towards them.

The Englishmen just had time to spring from their chairs and put themselves in front of the white girl before the foremost of the Turks were on them.

Immediately the Turks moved, the man on the couch by himself leapt to his feet.

Almost unnoticed in the confusion, he drew a revolver from his waist and fired twice at the chain of the lamp in his part of the room, bringing the lamp crashing down to the floor.

Then, in the semi-darkness, he leapt from the couch onto the backs of the Turks about the Europeans, throwing himself into the *mêlée*.

The semi-darkness which enveloped them was terrifying to the white girl. She could not see what was happening but the sounds of conflict before her made her crouch against the wall, half-fainting.

Confusion was greater in the gloom. Friend could scarcely be distinguished from foe in the jumbled crowd at the end of the room. Shouts and cries added to the clamour of conflict.

"The wall, Englishmen!—Door behind curtain—" a voice speaking English came hissingly through the clamour.

Suddenly, in the darkness, Daphnne felt herself touched—felt herself lifted from her feet with the utmost ease, held to a strong, easy-moving body, carried past a curtain, through a low, narrow archway, and out to the light of day.

She was dropped upon her feet, in pure, sweet air, in a box-like yard enclosed by four grey walls.

She had some idea that it was a Turk who had carried her from the café, for her cheek had rubbed a velvet jacket.

With suddenly warm cheeks she saw that it was—Conquest.

He sprang back to the door as the two Englishmen struggled through, and all three men put their strength against it, shutting it and barring it.

For a moment they paused to regain breath.

The young subaltern had lost his coat and his shirt was torn; Hadley, still holding his revolver, pressed his hankerchief to a knife-cut on his forehead; Conquest, in his Turkish dress, looked the least ruffled of the three.

He, the latter, had lost only his scarlet cap, and Daphnne, regarding him, thought his sleek, dark head looked European enough—and very youthful, very masterful.

He turned, crossed the yard to her where she stood breathing in the clear air. He bent a little—looked into her eyes.

"Experience is something not worth the price demanded for it," he said.

She dragged her look from his, flushing again. She was frightened still and angry—oh, infinitely angry.

"It's—it's fortunate you're so well known among the natives. You were able to help us knowing them and that place so well!"

Against one of the four walls an iron ladder was fixed. Conquest pointed to it.

"Climb up."

She looked up then.

Wide, glittering grey eyes met half-mocking, masterful hazel eyes. For a moment Daphnne hesitated, then, moving to the ladder, she climbed slowly up it. The men followed her.

They found themselves on the flat roof of the café.

Without pausing, Conquest led the way across the roofs of two other buildings. The last building ended on an alleyway. From this roof they dropped to the deserted side-street.

The girl had recovered from her fright but her slim little body quivered with angry feelings. She was glad enough to be out of the café but the way of her rescue was not at all to her liking.

The lithe, clean strength of those arms that had borne her from the café had been sweet enough then—but now she had time to remember to whom those strong arms belonged.

She had been carried with such ease . . . her immaculate loveliness had been held closely in a man's arms . . . pressed against a man's strongly beating heart. . . .

It was a hateful thing—to be rescued by just this one man. She could feel still those strong young arms about her—holding her with such ease!

She would not meet the mocking, masterful look in his bright golden eyes.

"Lord!" Stuart gasped. "That was a near thing—"

"It's very fortunate you chose that table at the end of the room," remarked Julian Conquest. "I don't know what would have been the end of that affair if you'd been somewhere else."

"Good Lord!" exclaimed Stuart. "Did you expect them to attack us like that?"

"I didn't know they were planning an outright

attack upon you, though I knew there was going to be some mischief there today. And I heard, also, that you were there."

He paused before he continued:

"I'm glad you took no notice of me. I dared not let you know I saw you. But what possessed you to go to such a place?" Conquest regarded the other two men. "You know its reputation—"

"But, hang it all, can't we go where we like?" exclaimed Stuart, flushing.

Conquest shrugged again.

"It isn't always wise. Those sort of places are best avoided. It saves a good deal of trouble. Until we're utterly sure of our position here—"

"But you, of course, go there," the girl's voice cut with sweet clearness above the men's tones.

Conquest's eyes gleamed.

"Yes," his voice was even deeper in tone, "but I don't go there as a European!"

"But why this planned attack upon us?" exclaimed Stuart. "It's not a thing they'd dare to do without good reason."

"I think there's very good reason," returned the other man, dragging his look from the girl's fair face, "when you consider that Miss Wayne and Captain Hadley are of a party who've come out here to get a certain man."

"By Gad!" exclaimed Hadley. "Do you think—"

"If either of you were missing, it would effectively stop Colonel Wayne in his work. And you play into their hands! You give them all the chance they want! It would be far better if you didn't go sight-seeing while with Colonel Wayne."

Captain Hadley accepted the reproof in silence. He was quite aware that they should not have gone to the café. But the slim, fair girl beside him had overruled all his wiser judgement.

"I understand, Conquest," he said after a moment. "We shall be more careful next time. We owe you some thanks—"

"Indeed, it's most fortunate for us that you know the East—the natives—so well," broke in Daphnne.

Julian Conquest's brown eyes glinted again. Her glance fell.

"It is," he said, and a moment later strode quickly up the street to find a car to convey them back to their small hotel.

* * *

As it was summer, the shutters of the hotel windows were open and a warm air, which smelt at its best of spices and sandalwood, came into the small rooms.

"Ah, *Mademoiselle*, I know that you would never be sorry if you visited my palace."

Ahmad Sueleman Bey bent his splendid form over the arm of his chair to speak to the girl who sat beside him.

Daphnne Wayne and the Bey sat in one of the small, but cool, rooms of the hotel.

"I have noticed, *Mademoiselle*, that you like beautiful things. Beauty sees beauty. So, *Mademoiselle*, I should like you to see my palace on the Syrian border. It is an Oriental palace, *Mademoiselle*, though I have, to the best of my ability, fitted it up with modern—what you say—luxuries."

Daphnne sat back in her easy-chair, her darkened lashes veiling her eyes, while the man beside her poured soft, attractive words into her quite ready ear.

"Oh, Bey, you make me want to see your palace. I wish we could pay you a visit."

Daphnne sat up and pushed back her fair curls.

"Is it not possible, *Mademoiselle?*" went on the man quickly, his glance upon those curls. "I am aware, *Mademoiselle*, that you are travelling to Aleppo and there intend parting with the *effendi* Wayne, your father. Is it not possible that, instead of going to Aleppo, you could journey down to my palace on the edge of the Syrian? Then, after a short stay, you might journey to Damascus to rejoin your friends, and the *effendi*, your father, could go on his way to Bagdad."

"I wonder if we could."

The Bey leant on the arm of his chair and looked down at the girl beside him. Of all the European women he had met he had never seen one more beautiful.

The green of her dress made her short hair gleam like bright gold, and her dark grey eyes had a dreamy look of expectancy.

A fair flower as yet unpicked ... a white rose untouched in the garden of the world ...

As she glanced up, he turned his head lest she should see the look in his eyes.

"Cannot you persuade the *effendi*, your father?"

"I'll try," she said, smiling.

The Bey, taking his leave a few minutes later, smiled with gratification.

And by that evening the plans were all settled. The Wayne party were to travel to Ahmad Sueleman Bey's palace while the Tennants journeyed to Damascus.

* * *

On the day before they were to leave, Colonel Wayne received a visitor in the form of the slim, dark, good-looking Lieutenant Conquest.

With characteristic directness the young Lieutenant came to the point:

"Colonel Wayne, I've heard that you intend visiting the palace of Ahmad Sueleman Bey."

"That's so."

"I've just come from the Consulate. They've sent me to advise you not to go to the Bey's palace."

"Eh?" Wayne regarded the younger man with surprise and enquiry.

"We have only lately learnt that the Bey has become your friend. We were very sorry to hear it."

"Why?" exclaimed the Colonel.

"You're not then aware," the hazel eyes beneath their dark, level brows returned the other man's look steadily, "that Ahmad Sueleman Bey is the man we suspect?"

"Ahmad Sueleman Bey!"

"The Bey is the man we have suspicions of. We believe him to be the man who's responsible for the disappearance of our men and the trouble here."

"Good God!" the Colonel exclaimed, and sat down to consider the matter.

44

The Bey was ruler of some small province. He was rich, powerful, influential. Wayne remembered his first meeting with the Bey in Constantinople. He had been brought to the hotel by Captain Price. And General Gayham had sent him; General Gayham, who had acknowledged him a friend!

As he thought, Colonel Wayne felt his suspicions unworthy, ridiculous. To suspect the Bey, the man who was doing his best to help them in the matter, who had already been of much assistance to them! As well to suspect one of themselves!

"That's ridiculous. You'll forgive me saying so, Lieutenant, but you're quite on the wrong track. Why, Sueleman Bey's the man who's helping us in the matter."

A faint smile curved the younger man's even lips.

"Does he help you very much?"

"Why, of course he does. At least he's doing his best."

"If he does, it's only to gain your confidence."

"Perhaps you're not aware that the Bey is a friend of General Gayham."

"We are aware of it," returned Conquest quietly. "The Bey makes a friend of all the English, in fact, in order to find out our plans."

"I can't believe it." The Colonel rose to his feet again.

"I'm sorry." There was sincere regret in the younger man's voice. "I was hoping you had some slight suspicion of the man."

Wayne looked hard at the man before him.

45

He was conscious of the other's good looks, his aloft carriage and slim grace.

Against his will be remembered his daughter's words—"He's a Turk." If only he could be sure. Was this man Conquest—or was he a Turk?

"I think you're quite wrong about Sueleman Bey. Have you any proof?"

"No." The other laughed, half-bitterly. "If we had, he wouldn't be at liberty to do the mischief he does."

"I really cannot believe you without some proof."

"At least, Colonel Wayne, give up all thought of going to his palace as you have planned."

"I can't do that. We're off tomorrow—"

"But your daughter, Miss Wayne—the risk for her—don't you see—?"

"If I thought there was the least risk in the matter," said Colonel Wayne quietly, "you may be sure I should not go."

"But, my God," there was no mistaking the vehemence in the young Lieutenant's tone, and his hazel eyes were wide and dark, "to us it's nothing less than a trap you're going into!"

"I can't believe that," the Colonel said sharply. "The Bey is our friend."

"But it's madness!"

Then, desperately, Conquest strove to control himself, to keep in check the fire of his Latin blood which was so quickly aroused.

"Colonel Wayne, is there nothing that will convince you, stop you going to the Bey's palace?"

"No, Lieutenant, I'm afraid there isn't. Sueleman Bey is our friend."

Weary and anxious at heart, the young Lieutenant slowly left the small hotel.

In the hotel entrance he met the Colonel's daughter.

Fate seemed pleased to bring together these two, the dark man and the fair girl, with their almost hostile feelings and youthful, unyielding wills.

She had been riding and in her plain white riding-suit looked almost a slim, lovely, golden-haired boy.

The man leant against the hotel doorway, looking down at her. He still believed her the pampered, spoilt child of civilisation, but since their first meeting his feelings towards her had changed somewhat.

The affair of the Café Orient was a pleasant memory. He had held her slim little body in his arms—and that could not be forgotten.

She was so fair to behold; surely she was fair of heart too. She had been indulged by father, friends, lovers; at heart she could not be utterly selfish.

And she was going with her father—was going to the palace of that Turk!

A stab of feeling like physical pain went through his heart.

For so long he had been fighting the East—striving to pierce its mystery—to outwit its cunning—and now the East was going to take this fair, lovely child, the only girl who had ever stirred his youthful blood.

Daphnne turned and saw him in the doorway —saw, too, the steady regard of his wide, hazel eyes, now no longer hard or mocking or arrogant but dark with a look that brought the colour to her cheeks.

They stood, regarding each other.

"Miss Wayne," he stepped down to the street, "I hear you are going to Ahmad Sueleman Bey's palace?"

"Yes, we're off tomorrow." She tilted her fair head, giving him a provocative, almost challenging look.

Although she strove not to be aware of his face, she was half-afraid of this slim, dark young man. She never felt very safe or very sure of herself in his presence as in the presence of other men. He was so good-looking, so masterful.

He stirred her in some strange and powerful way quite new to her. And she felt herself responding in a way that, to her, was quite alarming.

She felt that if he exerted that strange power he had, she would have no will to resist him. And to Daphnne, who always had her own way, this was quite disturbing.

"Daphnne!" He moved suddenly, took her hands in his. "Don't go to this Bey's palace! We don't trust him. Don't go."

She stood mute, held by the clasp of his slender fingers, strong and warm about her own— the look in his wide golden eyes that gazed down into hers.

"Daphnne, don't go to his palace!"

He had drawn her a little towards him and she felt quite incapable of resisting. Her slim form was almost against his—his warm breath came upon her lips as he slowly bent to her—

With a faint gasp she got command of herself, dragged her hands from his, started back.

A sweet, potent emotion that was utterly new to her had held her almost passive.

Subconsciously she was aware that his embrace would have given her keen pleasure—but she could not give in to him—could not yield.

"Lieutenant Conquest!" She panted and strove to put all the coldness she could command into her voice.

"Daphnne—" he pleaded.

Daphnne put herself on the entrance step, above him.

"Lieutenant Conquest—I don't understand you. The Bey is our friend. I shall certainly go to his palace."

The man's eyes darkened.

"Miss Wayne," he restrained himself, spoke slowly, "it is not safe for you to go. We believe Ahmad Sueleman Bey to be a lawless and unscrupulous Turk—the man responsible for the trouble here."

"The Bey?" She half-frowned. "Oh, but he's our friend."

"A false friend, Miss Wayne. If you went to his palace I know that you would regret it."

"Really, I can't believe that."

"Miss Wayne, you do not know the East. You have only seen it outwardly—mystic, picturesque. But beneath the surface it is not beautiful. The Café Orient is but a slight revelation of what it can be."

At the mention of the Café Orient, Daphnne flushed. He reminded her of just the one thing she wished to forget. Reminded her that she had been held in his arms.

"You don't seem to mind it," she returned. "You seemed pretty used to it in that Oriental place."

"Because my work takes me into it. It's hateful to think of you going into that darker East. I cannot think of your fair beauty at the mercy of the East!"

His brown eyes were again wide and intense —his voice almost passionate. Daphnne strove to cling to her assurance, her anger.

"Miss Wayne," he moved to the entrance step, "won't you believe me when I say you'd be in danger if you went to this Turk's palace? Won't you give up all thought of going and try to persuade your father not to go?"

"Lieutenant Conquest, the Bey is our friend."

The man drew back. A brightness showed suddenly in his golden eyes—the glint of anger.

"Perhaps when you are in his palace you'll find out your mistake!" he returned with sudden hardness and curtness.

"Well, I certainly shan't dissuade Father after persuading him to go!"

She heard the faint catch of his breath, saw the flash of his brown eyes.

So she was responsible, he thought; responsible for the Englishmen giving themselves into the hands of the Turk! Responsible for this mad journey to the Bey's palace!

"Are you so utterly blind to your danger?" he exclaimed furiously.

"I may remind you we can judge for ourselves when danger lies for us."

"If you find yourself in a Turkish harem, perhaps you'll understand your foolishness!"

Her grey eyes opened wide, and then she laughed.

"Oh, Lieutenant Conquest, you're most amusing!" she cried. "You may be sure *I* shan't enter any Eastern harem."

With that she turned and went into the hotel, a slim, attractive, assured little figure.

The man, his slender hands clenched at his sides and passion still gleaming in his golden eyes, strode off from the hotel and up the street, also a slim, attractive, and masterful figure.

Chapter Four

Down a rough winding road into more wooded country three cars were travelling at the best speed that the rough going would allow.

In the first and most luxurious car travelled the Bey and Colonel Wayne and his daughter; the following car held Captain Hadley, Lieutenant Marsh, and a Turk of the Bey, and the third car had the Colonel's four men.

Daphnne's maid had refused to accompany her mistress at the last moment. Not even the chance of losing her position had made her alter her decision. So Daphnne, who did not mind very much, accompanied the men alone.

To the Europeans that journey by car was an exceedingly long one. On the Colonel remarking upon the distance, the Bey assured them that they had not much farther to go and vowed that the vile roads, which caused such wearisome travelling for Europeans, made the journey seem double its actual length.

"*Mademoiselle*, I am desolate. You must be wearied to utter fatigue." The Bey bent forward, all consideration, to address the fair girl who, in her neat white costume and white hat, leant back in one corner of the car.

Daphnne looked up into the Turk's black eyes.

"No, Bey, I'm not too tired. All this journey is interesting to me."

As the sun was nearing the western horizon, the cars, travelling through slightly wooded country, came down a sloping way to a dark, quick-moving river.

"*Effendi*, yonder lies my palace."

Sueleman Bey, with a graceful gesture, waved his hand towards the trees on the far bank.

The following car, in which were the Captain and the Lieutenant, came up.

The girl and the Englishman looked about them. It was a fair enough place, wild, luscious, tropical. On the far bank was a large wooden hut and on the water before this hut floated what appeared to be a huge raft.

The Europeans and the Turk had been talking for some minutes but no third car had appeared. The Bey was all consideration.

"Trouble of the engine, maybe. My man driving could not possibly miss the way. Something delayed them. Will you wait, *effendi?*"

"If you think they're coming along all right, we'll go on, Bey," said the Colonel. "But—how do we cross?"

The Bey stood up and signalled across the river, but already the big raft-like construction was being propelled across the water by three natives.

It grated against a properly erected landing-stage on the bank a short distance from the waiting cars.

They Bey's driver immediately sent the car onto the landing-stage and from there onto the raft. Then the natives pushed off, taking the car across the river.

The water curled dark and strong about the raft. By the banks it moved almost sluggishly. In the water by one bank a long, dark shape rose above the surface and then disappeared amidst small waves.

The white girl, looking from the car, attracted the men's attention to it with a faint exclamation.

"Good Gad!" exclaimed the Colonel. "Crocodiles? I didn't know they came in this part."

The Bey shrugged and spread his hands while his black eyes sleepily regarded the river.

"But a few, *effendi*. They come, at times, in this water."

"But isn't it a bit awkward for you having the things here, Bey?"

"But no, *effendi*. I have no trouble with them." The Bey smiled. "There is no danger—if you get not in the water."

The raft was pushed against the farther bank and the car purred off onto another landing-stage beside the hut.

Again the raft was propelled across the water and the second car was brought over the river in the same way as the first.

No third car had appeared.

The Bey's car travelled through the trees for a short way and then, coming out to a cleared part of the land, slowed down and the Europeans saw before them a wide, rambling, but walled, village with a fair villa or palace in the centre.

At first glance the Bey's palace appeared an attractive, picturesque spot.

It appeared of three large wings with a domed roof in the centre. The green of the trees made the palace and mosque show up with arresting paleness though the sinking sun threw rays of gold over all.

"It's lovely!" exclaimed the girl in the car.

"I must say; you've got a pretty fair place here, Bey," added the Englishman.

"I am overjoyed." The Turk bent his fine form forward and made a quick gesture with his hands. "My poor home finds favour in your eyes."

The car carried them swiftly down to the gate and into the large village.

Through a dark, jostling crowd of people, carts and wagons, horses, bullocks, mules and goats, the Bey's car was driven slowly to the palace in the centre.

As they approached it, the beauty of the palace became more distinct to the Europeans. Beautiful at a distance, it was a yet more lovely building at near sight.

Through iron gates into a paved courtyard before the palace the cars purred and came to a stop.

The Bey alighted and assisted his English guests from the car. He led the way up the entrance steps, through an elaborate arched entrance, and into the cool, fragrant hall.

"Welcome to my palace!" said the Turk.

*   *   *

A mingled fragrance of sandalwood and incense, of rose and jasmine, and the faint sweet sound of bells ringing awoke Daphnne Wayne on the morning following the day she and her father had arrived at the palace.

She sat curled up on the huge bed and with wide grey eyes regarded the attractive splendour of the chamber she was in. The beauty, the Eastern splendour of the luxuriousness of it, held the white girl spellbound.

Here was the East that she had wished to see; the East that was serene, gorgeous, entrancing. Yet the very beauty, the alluring, voluptuous atmosphere, stirred in her a strange unrest and uneasiness.

She had longed to be in the beautiful East, but now that she was in it, it stirred a greater longing in her heart. She sat on the wide bed and clasped her knees. Remembrance of the night before came back to her. She had a vivid impression of it.

They had sat on soft ottomans and had their dinner on small tables in company with the Bey.

The entrance of two soft-footed Turkish girls into her chamber startled Daphnne from her thoughts.

One was lightly clad and veiled, the other wore long trousers and embroidered jacket. They bowed to her in Oriental fashion.

One drew aside the gold curtains and pushed back the shutters which hid the terrace, letting rays of golden sunlight into the gorgeous apartment.

The other girl brought into the room a tray with coffee, rolls, creamy butter, and a bowl of fresh, luscious fruit.

With a faint laugh Daphnne picked up the blooms and regarded them.

Later, when she had bathed in the cool bathroom adjoining the bedchamber, the girls brought soft, elegant garments and placed them on the bed.

Daphnne asked for her travelling-trunk, but both girls shook their heads.

"Hasn't it come? Hasn't the car arrived?" she exclaimed, but the girls shook their heads again.

Daphnne half-frowned. She preferred her own things, though everything she wanted had been brought for her. The girls held up the garments they had brought. Daphnne glanced at them. They were soft, exquisite things but diaphanous for all their elegance.

She shook her head and pointed to her own white European costume.

The girls tried to persuade her but Daphnne would not be persuaded to make any change of dress and put on her own white things.

The room which led from the bedchamber was but a larger replica of the other chamber—just as gorgeous, just as attractive.

The terrace went the length of both apartments and Daphnne stepped out beneath the jasmine and roses to the warm sunlight. Below her a fair garden lay, exquisite in the brilliant day.

She stepped back into the room as Sueleman Bey entered the apartment.

The Turk had changed from the somewhat pompous but exceedingly courteous personage in the braided uniform who had driven with them the day before.

He was more the Oriental now, and, in his own palace, more commanding. A robe of green

silk clothed his tall, splendid figure, long trousers
were tightened in at the ankle, and Oriental slippers with curled toes were on his feet, and his
face looked darker and handsome.

He moved across the room with a soft, graceful step, his look fixed upon the white girl with
a strange brightness and intentness.

Daphnne experienced again that feeling of
uneasiness—fear, almost—that she had felt before
in his presence.

"Ah, *Mademoiselle*, I have been all anxiety
to know how you feel. My people have waited
upon you? These rooms please you?"

His soft voice instantly soothed the girl's disturbed feelings. She answered at once:

"Oh, Bey, no-one could complain of your
hospitality. And these rooms are perfectly lovely."

"Then you are comfortable here?" His black
eyes looked down at her with eager light.

"Could anyone be anything else in such an
extremely lovely place! But, Bey, I'm in want of
my trunk. Has the other car arrived with father's
men and the luggage?"

There was a faint flicker of the heavy lashes
over the black eyes, but the girl did not notice.

"*Mademoiselle*, I am desolated. I have been—
what you say—very busy since my return. I do not
know if the *effendi*'s car has arrived. But, *Mademoiselle*, I will make enquire."

"Thanks, Bey. You see," she laughed lightly,
"I feel rather lost without my luggage."

"You like my palace, *Mademoiselle?*" he murmured after a while.

"I think it is a most lovely place."

"*Mademoiselle*, you make me happy," murmured the Turk, and his dark eyes gleamed beneath their heavy lids. "I have come to show you a little more of the palace and the garden round it."

Through wide, gorgeous chambers in the left wing of the palace, in which were her apartments, the Turk took Daphnne. By certain doors they passed through, big natives stood motionless and silent as statues.

"Do you keep a guard about the palace, Bey?" she laughingly asked the man beside her.

"*Mademoiselle*, this is the East," returned the Turk.

Daphnne did not pursue the subject. She was aware, since she had been in the palace, that the Bey, for all his praise of Western ways, was Oriental in his way of life in his own home.

From a jasmine-hung terrace they went down white steps to the palace garden.

A wave of perfume, the perfume from a thousand flowers and tropical plants, enveloped them, sweet, heavy, overwhelming. . . .

To the white girl that garden was the most beautiful she had ever seen. She scarcely heard the murmured words of the man beside her; her eyes and her senses were drugged with the beauty that surrounded her. . . .

"You like it, my garden?" enquired the Turk, softly.

"Oh, it is lovely," murmured the girl. "In such a place as this you must be awfully happy, Bey. I should think here you must have everything you could possibly desire."

"Everything but my Heart's Desire may be here—yet I may not—yet—possess it."

The man raised a trailing branch in order that his tall, silk-clad form could pass beneath an arch, and scattered soft, fragrant petals over the girl.

"*Mademoiselle*, it is cool here by the lake."

Daphnne went beside the Turk down white steps to a paved walk before a mirror-like lake. A stone seat was facing the water and the man moved forward to arrange gorgeous cushions upon it for her.

The girl leant back on the wide seat, her lissom, white-clad figure relaxed against the cushions. Softly, on slippered feet, the man moved along the back of the seat.

Daphnne sat entranced by the exquisite scene before her. The lake was like a quivering mirror in its frame of marble. She felt her senses drugged by the beauty of it all. . . . The scent of all the flowers was heavy, overpowering. . . .

Her eyes closed. The warmth and the stillness, the sweet, heavy scent, the faint sound of bells—held her senses as in a spell.

A man's caressing hands touched her shoulders . . . her arms. . . .

"Of all the flowers in my garden, thou art the most fair! Thou art the loveliest flower in all the world."

Daphnne opened her eyes and strove to sit up. Breaking through that delicious, languorous spell there came a surging, throbbing sense of unrest.

Slowly she remembered the Turk's presence. She was not sure if she had really felt a man's caressing hands touching her, and she had not noted the Bey's words, but his soft voice murmuring at her shoulder made her aware of his presence. She struggled to her feet from the cushioned seat.

"Your—your garden is too beautiful, Bey." Her voice was a little unsteady and she strove desperately to command herself. "Take me back to the palace."

Daphnne moved away from the lake and back up the steps. Softly, with a graceful step, the Bey followed her.

"I have yet something more to show you, *Mademoiselle*," said the Turk.

*   *   *

Daphnne frowned a little as she stood by the centre couch in the largest room of her apartment.

She could not understand the strange spell that had stolen about her in the palace garden. Her heart still throbbed with an unusual heaviness.

The Bey entered the apartment.

Behind him came two native attendants, each bearing an artistic gilt box.

At a sign from their master they placed the boxes on the big couch and went silently from the room.

"*Mademoiselle*, do you like jewels?"

"Jewels?"

Sueleman Bey leant over the couch and flung up the lid of first one box and then the other.

Daphnne gasped. From one box, gleaming, dazzling lights twinkled and sparkled; from the other came a white, brilliant sheen.

Jewels! Daphnne had never seen such jewels before, and jewels massed in such careless confusion.

"Look—*Mademoiselle!*"

The Turk dipped his dark hands into the pale,

gleaming lustre in one box and lifted up pearls. Pearls whose pale, flawless beauty made the girl catch her breath.

"Oh, Bey—how lovely!"

"Pearls, pale, pure—they were made for the whiteness—the beauty—of European women."

Daphnne fingered heavy rope of creamy whiteness. The gleaming surface of the pearls slipped softly between her hands.

The Bey dipped his hands into the other box and scattered the jewels out on the couch.

"Look—*Mademoiselle*."

She regarded the gems, amazed, entranced.

The Turk watched her. His black eyes were gleaming with scarcely paler light than the jewels on the couch.

In the world of the West, men would fight and kill—for their possession! In the Western world, such jewels were rarely seen. They were the product, the wealth, of the Orient.

"Why—they must be worth a fortune!" whispered the white girl.

The Turk took a step towards her.

"They shall be yours!" he said. "All yours—if you wish!"

Slowly Daphnne raised her eyes from the jewels; eyes that were wide, almost blank in expression.

"Mine?"

Daphnne came slowly out of the spell the jewels had set upon her.

For the first time she became aware of the gleam in the Turk's black eyes—his heavy breaths —the quiver of his dark, well-shaped hands—

"Yes, yes. All shall be yours. My wealth, my power! All I lay at your feet!"

Daphnne took a step back. She had seen passion in the eyes of men, but the passion which showed now in the Turk's eyes held her mute for a moment.

"What do you mean?"

"Ah, cannot you understand, fair rose of the West—cannot you understand?" Passion gleamed in Sueleman Bey's black eyes and sounded in the heaviness of his voice.

"I offer you—all I possess. I offer you half the wealth of the Orient; the power of a Sultan. All I offer if you will—come to me—marry me."

"Marry you!"

Daphnne's grey eyes dilated, darkened to a shade of purple-grey.

"Yes," exclaimed the Turk, "I ask you to marry me!"

The heavy rope of pearls slipped from the girl's fingers to the floor. Her small, white-clad figure leant back against the couch.

This Turk, who was their friend, who had ever been the suave, courteous Oriental, wanted to marry her!

All the time that she had accepted him as a friend he had been regarding her with eyes that were not those of a friend—had been desiring her—

Passion fired Sueleman Bey. He saw no further need for restraint.

"Ah, Desire of my Heart, at last I may speak. At last I may say to you how I worship—how I adore you! When my eyes first beheld you, a flame of fire was lit within my breast—the desire of a man aroused within my heart! A vision of loveliness, you may have filled my thoughts in the day and my dreams in the long, dark hours of night till my longing and desire tortured—"

"Bey . . . please stop!"

The white girl backed again but the man, with Eastern passion, went on:

"The desire of my days was to have you in my palace. I longed to give you the ease of life here— flowers to drug you to sleep with their perfume— the pleasure of desires fulfilled—the delight of love—"

"Bey . . ."

"Thou wouldst be the most precious of all my possessions, for I adore thee!" cried the Turk, his hands held out to touch her.

With an inarticulate cry Daphnne sprang round the couch, putting it between them.

"Will you stop!" she cried. "What you ask is impossible."

Anger showed in the sparkle of her grey eyes, and this, more than anything else, checked the man, put a rein to his passion that was beginning to master him.

The Turk drew back.

"What did you say?"

"I said that what you ask is impossible. I could not even think of it."

Sueleman Bey stared in amazement; amazement with fury behind it.

"Do you mean," he cried, "that you refuse me?"

"Of course. I couldn't consider such a thing as you suggest."

"You refuse me!" he cried.

It seemed that the Turk could not believe what she said. And, indeed, he could not. That she had refused him! Refused him—Ahmad Sueleman Bey! He who had never asked anything of a woman before—he who had commanded!

"So—you refuse me!" cried Sueleman Bey.

"I do!" returned the white girl, her grey eyes glittering angrily, her gold curls tossed back.

Fury gleamed in the Turk's black eyes.

All the arrogance and pride of his race showed in his look. And she had scorned it; had, in his eyes, dragged his pride in the dust.

Fury surged in Sueleman Bey. Desperately he strove for control over himself, for calmness.

The innate cruelty of the man was aroused by her words, by her stiff little figure.

He longed to grip her—to crush her in his hands—to hurt her physically—and yet he did not dare—he did not dare to harm that fair beauty that he so fiercely desired!

Slowly the Turk mastered himself. Slowly his black eyes narrowed; a faint smile parted his full lips—a smile that deepened the girl's uneasiness.

"*Mademoiselle*," his voice was again suave and soft, if a little deeper in tone, "I have something more that I wish to show to you. Will you please to come with me, *Mademoiselle?*"

Sueleman Bey led the way from the left wing of the palace, across the splendid hall, and into the right wing. Through elegant apartments, up richly carpeted stairs, and across quiet passages he went, and stopped at an alcove before a small window.

Bending slightly, he looked out the window

while the girl behind him waited in some surprise.

"Look, *Mademoiselle.*"

Softly the Turk backed from the window, a smile curling back his full lips, his eyes gleaming between their heavy lashes.

With deeper surprise and faint uneasiness Daphnne stepped up to the window.

Looking down, she could see part of a paved courtyard which ended in a flower-filled garden. As she looked, men appeared, walking across the courtyard; natives in robes and jackets, a tall man in white—

Almost immediately Daphnne recognised her father, with his stiff, upright carriage, grey-gold head—

A faint cry escaped her. Colonel Wayne was in the midst of the Turks, his wrists bound behind him!

Even as the girl saw this, the sound of a scuffle, sudden cries, drew her attention behind the Colonel.

Captain Hadley, his white coat torn, his fair hair all disordered, was being dragged forward, struggling furiously despite bound hands.

Last came a third European, also bound. Lieutenant Marsh, resisting and exclaiming, as he was drawn along in the midst of dark Turks.

Resisting, the white men were dragged across the courtyard by their dark captors, then vanished from sight within the palace, and all again was quiet.

Daphnne Wayne leant against the wall by the window. She felt cold, stiff. For a moment she was petrified.

A soft, flower-scented wind came in through

the opening and lifted the gold curls about her face. She swung round and faced the Turk.

"What does this mean?" she gasped.

Sueleman Bey laughed—mocking, triumphant laughter.

Suddenly, as a blinding revelation, the truth leapt up before Daphnne.

"You are the Turk my father's come to get—"

Sueleman Bey folded his arms on his broad breast.

"I," he said, "am the Turk!"

Chapter Five

Daphnne Wayne was scarcely aware of her return to her own apartment. She felt stunned by the knowledge, by the revelation of the truth.

Sueleman Bey, the Turk they wanted!

He had vowed himself ready in every way to assist the Englishmen in revealing and bringing to justice the man who was plotting secretly against them—and he himself was the man!

The revelation held the white girl speechless. Slowly, as one recovers from unconsciousness, she recovered from the astounding knowledge, deliberately forcing herself to realise the truth.

They had been warned. She recalled suddenly the warning she had received from Conquest— the one man she could not forget. She remembered that she had laughed then. But *he* had been right—

She swung round, facing him with tightly clenched hands, with small figure rigid and eyes bright as shadowed steel.

"So you are the Turk. You—the man who professed the sincerest friendship for us!"

"I—am the Turk!" There was cool arrogance

in the way Sueleman Bey answered. "The cold, foolish English were, oh, so easily deceived!"

"They'll not be always deceived! You'll find that out to your cost!"

The Bey shrugged mockingly and the green silk shimmered on his broad shoulders.

"Do you think you'll be allowed to act in this way?" Anger brought a flush to her face, made her grey eyes sparkle. "Do you think you can keep us here, prisoners in your palace! My father, my friends—"

The Turk laughed mockingly.

"You will stay in my palace for as long as it does please me!"

"You are ridiculous!" exclaimed Daphnne— Daphnne, the petted child of civilisation, whose beauty and position had always given her perfect freedom.

"Why can I not keep you here?" The Turk folded his arms on his breast and looked down at her, supreme in his power.

Daphnne caught her breath. In his dark eyes she saw again the smouldering passion and it frightened her despite her spirit and her pride.

"Do you know who we are?" she cried. "My father is Colonel Wayne."

"Yes, O Flower of Delight. Should I have taken so much trouble to be sure of his arrival at my palace if he had not been the Colonel Wayne?"

"But—" She gasped. "Do you know our people will be out searching for us?"

Softly Sueleman Bey laughed.

"They will not find you."

"Not find us! You're ridiculous. My father will be searched for all over the country!"

"Searched for, perhaps—but not found. 'Tis true your English friends knew you were coming to my palace, but they thought you were coming as guests to me.

"It will be some time before they are curious as to where you are. And in that time, O Woman of my Desire, thou wilt have known the delight of love—the joy of wondrous hours possessed! When they become curious, then they may not find you, for my palace is not known to them."

Daphnne put a small hand against her throat. The man's words sent a chill to her heart; held her speechless despite the anger which surged in her.

She remembered the warning they had received against this very man!

"You must be mad! Do you think you can keep us prisoners here in your palace?" She faced him still, proud, furious.

"Listen, thou pale woman of a cold, arrogant race." He took a step towards her. "'Tis not for a little thing that I have planned. The cool, interfering English shall fall beneath a power greater than they! They shall be driven from this country!"

A faint cry left the girl's lips.

She had never taken much interest in the affair which had brought her father to Turkey. Seeking her own pleasures, she had never troubled about the matter upon which the Englishmen were unceasingly working.

Now, in all its seriousness, it was revealed to her. She not only saw it but realised how great were the Turk's plans, how great the peril of the English in that unreliable country.

The realisation brought a cry from her lips.

The Turk who had once been a suave, courteous friend now appeared a monster of vileness—from whom she instinctively shrank.

The peril of the Englishmen whitened her cheeks. She had been an indulged, pleasure-loving child without a care in the world, yet it seemed to her in that moment that she became a woman—a woman realising that life was not all a game but something serious, terrifying.

Sueleman Bey looked down at her with gleaming dark eyes. He took a step towards her.

White and stiff she stood, and he took yet another step nearer.

"And your master also will I be!" His voice came hissingly as he lowered it, let the passion slip a little from it. "Master of you—of your fair form—your white beauty—of your life—"

"Never!" Daphnne gasped furiously.

"You shall learn the customs here. You shall know the life of one of my women!" went on the Turk. "In the madness of my desire I would have spared the Englishmen a little longer and made you my favourite. You refused me! You shall know how I repay refusal—from a white woman! Now you shall live as the woman of a Turk!"

Rage held Daphnne speechless.

"Never!" she gasped at last.

Sueleman Bey walked softly on slippered feet towards the door.

"Meditate on what I have said, little white rose."

With that the Turk stepped swiftly and silently from the chamber.

* * *

While the brilliant yellow sun travelled slowly yet surely westward across the sky, Daphnne Wayne sat facing the awful truth of their position.

Ahmad Sueleman Bey had got them into his power; had succeeded in his cunning scheme.

The result of his capture of them the girl did not like to consider. She knew now how great were his plans. Their capture might affect the whole country.

Swiftly, involuntarily, a cry left the girl's lips. In that moment she remembered what had, perhaps, been the fate of the other Englishmen at the hands of this Turk.

They had never been heard of again, and that could only mean—death. Death! Was this to be the fate of her father—her friends?

White-faced, with dilated eyes, Daphnne sprang to her feet. Was that to be the fate of the three men she had seen being dragged, prisoners, across the courtyard?

"Oh, God, not that!" she cried.

And her own fate—what was that to be? Remembering the look in the Turk's eyes, she crouched, cold with horror, on the splendour of the cushions.

Surely they would be searched for?

Besides the Tennants, the English in the towns they had left knew they were going to the Bey's palace. But would they come in time? Would they come in time to save her father and friends—to save her?

There was one man who might come to their help. Julian Conquest had been the last to warn

72

them. He might suspect something and come to their assistance.

Daphnne knew that if he was determined to find them, he would—and the knowledge stirred her crushed spirit, brought a warmth to her heart that was like exulting fire.

But would he? Agonising doubt seized her. She remembered their last meeting.

She had laughed at his warning. She had met him with hostility that she had shown to no other man. They had parted more enemies than friends, each arrogant, each proud in their youth and their will.

He might not care now—if she suffered. He might let her go. . . .

Daphnne, shivering on the voluptuous cushions, realised that she was responsible. Colonel Wayne would not have come to the Bey's palace if she hadn't persuaded him.

Daphnne, the light-hearted, pleasure-loving child of civilisation, realised, for the first time in her life, the cost to others of the gratification of her own desires.

She had brought her father, her friends, perhaps to their death. The realisation sent her sobbing and shivering into the soft midst of the cushions.

The sun sank towards the western horizon and a glow of gold settled over the land.

Daphnne Wayne sat up and smoothed back the curls which were a fair, tumbled mess about her head.

The approach of night terrified her.

With the setting of the sun the Bey came to

her and Daphnne summoned up all that was left of her spirit of the morning to meet him.

"Has my flower of flowers meditated upon my words of the early day?"

The Turk, a splendid figure in a robe of yellow silk adorned in front with pearls, moved softly across the carpeted floor.

"Do you not see, Delight of my Heart, how useless it is to resist? Behold, the night comes—a night of magic, shadowed, throbbing hours—for love! Let there be no more anger. Come willingly to my arms—"

Daphnne faced him, standing almost rigid by the couch.

"No!"

The Turk moved up to her. Slowly her grey eyes dilated; she went back, gasping a little. In his look she saw what she had not seen in the eyes of other men. She was woman enough to understand.

The naked facts of life were before her. Here life was unveiled—savage—menacing. She was caught now—forced to understand its merciless reality.

All that his look conveyed to her held her mute and stiff with horror.

"You are foolish," he said softly, and smiled a little. "Do you not see how useless it is to say 'No'? I have more strength than you—in all ways. I have desired you for long—and I will have what I want—"

Daphnne closed her eyes, striving to fight off the awful dread which chilled her heart and body.

"Will you not see how vain is your resistance?" he said, his ardent gaze on her shrinking form. "Soon—or late—you will have to surrender. Submit now, without all this useless and foolish fight."

He put out a dark hand to touch her—but with an inarticulate ejaculation she shrank against the couch.

"Let there be no more unkind words to me," he said. "Come to my arms—and know the joy of living—the sweet delight—"

Faint colour came back to her pale cheeks.

"No!"

His dark glance flickered over her slim, light-clad figure—and to the girl his look was like a flame travelling over her chilled body.

"If you would but sleep one night within my arms—"

"You beast!" she panted. "I loathe you!"

He smiled. Her resistance, her passion, added fuel to the fire of his hot blood—increased his fierce desire for conquest, for possession—

"Foolish little English flower," said the Turk. "Still so proud, so arrogant. Yet soon you will admit defeat to me. Those soft lips that speak such angry words to me—will rest upon mine . . . those pale hands now so tightly closed—will caress me. . . ."

"Never!" she gasped. "If I'm harmed here—the English'll make you pay without mercy—"

"You repulse me—you throw your scorn at me," cried the Turk, "yet have you forgotten that you and the Englishmen are in my power?"

Forgotten! Daphnne drew a swift breath through her set teeth. As if she could forget!

Watching her, the Turk saw dark fear in the girl's dilated eyes—and his own narrowed.

"You defy me, yet have you forgotten that I hold life—or death—for the Englishmen?"

A faint, very faint, cry escaped her then, and she swayed back slightly.

Smiling, Sueleman Bey turned towards the door.

"I am patient—yet my patience will not endure forever. A little more time shall you have to reconsider your answer to me. Remember, I have the fate of the Englishmen in my hands!"

When he had gone, Daphnne flung herself against the door but with its perfect mechanism it had shut and locked.

Daphnne, for the first time in her life, knew what terror the night could bring—knew with what agonising slowness the still, dusky hours could drag their wearying course. . . .

Fully dressed, she lay sleepless on the silken pillows of the big bed in the inner room—till the pearly light of dawn forced its way between the gilt shutters and into the apartment.

Because their position was desperate—she attempted to escape.

Knotting together the costly cloths and draperies which were spread over the bed, she fastened one end to the white parapet of the terrace and let herself down this gorgeous swaying rope—down into the arms of the Turk's men waiting beneath the terrace!

Tasting the bitterness of failure, she was taken back to the palace—back to her apartment. Daphnne leant against a pillar of the terrace, shivering, panting a little.

Softly but swiftly Sueleman Bey entered the

chamber, and she turned, facing him with the look of a creature at bay.

"You little fool!" he said harshly. "Do you not yet know that there is no escape from me?"

Daphnne pressed her hands against the pillar behind her; only the heave of her breast betrayed the wild unrest within her.

"I have come for my answer," he said. "What have you to say? Do you agree—?"

"No, no—never!"

"It is not my will to be patient," he said. "How much longer are you going to keep me waiting?"

"I'll never agree!" she cried. "Nothing you can say or do will ever make me alter my decision. I loathe you!"

The Turk's eyes gleamed; a flush of passion mounted to his dark face.

"Must I show you you're here for my pleasure! —my slave!" he snarled, and towered over her, furious, menacing.

Even then she still faced him.

"You," cried the man, "shall learn submission! You shall know my power. You shall be lashed if you will not obey my commands. You shall know I am master here."

He moved—caught hold of her and flung her upon the couch.

She fell heavily on the cushions; yet, with the swiftness of youth, she writhed over, off them, tumbling them upon the floor, and his hand touched only her shoulder as he bent to her, dragging one side of the silken jumper off, marking the whiteness of her soft flesh.

Gaining her feet, she sprang away, but one

of the cushions made her stumble and the Turk caught her, crushed her in his arms.

However, Sueleman Bey had not before held in his arms a white woman—a white woman who resisted. She was out of his arms almost as swiftly as she was in them.

"You little white tigress!" he cried.

"You beast!" she flung at him. "You shall pay for this. You'll pay with your life—to the English!"

The Turk sprang towards her again. With a faint cry she eluded him and fled from the chamber up to the long terrace. Her back to the low, wide parapet, she faced him.

"Stop! If you come near—if you touch me— I'll throw myself down!"

"Into the arms of my men?" cried the Turk, mockingly.

Daphnne swung round, then looked down. Beneath the terrace were the Turks, half-a-dozen of the Bey's men, squatting and lounging in indolent attitudes.

With a gasping breath she shrank back, and the Bey caught her from behind and dragged her off the terrace in his arms.

She struggled with the fury of desperation. Yet, with a numbing terror, she felt herself utterly powerless in the Turk's hold.

All her remaining strength she had put into that first, fierce fight with him. She felt now helpless ... exhausted ... almost on the verge of fainting. . . .

She felt his gripping hands; saw his dark, passion-flushed face above her own . . . his eyes gleaming with desire . . . his sensuous lips seeking hers. . . .

Daphnne screamed—screamed shrilly and almost involuntarily.

It disturbed the Turk, pierced through the haze of his passion. He half-released her and she slipped, fainting, to the rug at his feet.

Sueleman Bey strove to put some control upon himself, though passion, desire, still gleamed in his eyes.

"I am weary of waiting. You shall obey—you shall submit! You shall give in to my will!"

With that he turned and walked across the floor to the panelled door.

* * *

When Daphnne recovered consciousness she found herself in the harem.

Her impressions of her experiences there were vague. Vague impressions of horror, of terror, of humiliation.

There, Turkish women had stripped her of her European clothes, bathed her in a perfumed bath, and attired her in scanty garments of the Orient.

She had fought; with all the fury of a proud, unbending spirit and the strength of a supple young body, she had resisted.

But the eunuch who had carried her to the harem was a muscular giant and the women who carried out the Turk's orders were five in number, so that, with all her rage and unyielding will, she found her frantic efforts of resistance useless.

From the harem she had been carried back to her apartment in the left wing.

Then had followed paralysing terror. Throughout the night she had shivered in the hot, close air of the rooms. But the Turk did not come to her. Throbbing moments of terror—dragging hours of sickening dread.

Through the golden day that followed, another night, and yet another day, she waited in her lovely rooms in an agony of suspense.

Yet the Turk made no move.

She did not know it was but a little thing kept the Turk from her—saved her in those passing hours—the arrival of his son at the palace.

Moving restlessly as she sat on the big couch in the largest room of the apartment, Daphnne looked down at the scanty garments that clothed her—and again warm colour stung her cheeks and rage and terror warred within her.

She was utterly lovely in the light dress of the East. The scantiness of the dainty, elegant, Oriental clothes showed an exquisite outline of form.

Waist, arms, and throat showed bare and pale with the paleness of a Western skin. A white veil, fastened to her head, lay over her slender body like a diaphanous cloud and showed, as through a mist, the silken gold of her hair.

Dragging the diaphanous veil round her, Daphnne started up from the couch and walked to the terrace. The air was so hot—the fumes of incense made her feel faint.

She felt she could endure no more. The end would come soon now. She did not allow herself to think of what had happened to her father and friends. And there seemed no chance of help, of rescue for them.

Starting forward, she reached the cool, white parapet and leaning against it threw back her head to let the faint, sweet wind come coolly upon her face and throat and breast.

A little below her was the palace garden. She looked down at it.

Suddenly she drew herself up stiff against the parapet.

Looking down, she saw a man come through the trees and flowering bushes of the garden. He was young, slim, lithe of movement, swinging of step. A robe of yellow silk shimmered on his supple, athletic form, and an orange sash was tight about his waist.

As masterful and as richly attired as the Bey, yet he was more attractive with his youth and his slim grace.

She knew him—knew him immediately her glance was on him. Unerring instinct told her who it was, though reason strove, unsuccessfully, to deny it.

Seeing him, the warm blood seemed to stir in her stiff body—to throb in her throat, to burn in her cheeks. The sight of this one man brought the pulsating, potent life back to her; raised her almost-crushed spirit from its humiliation.

Her faint cry brought one of the Turkish girls swiftly to her side.

"Who is—he?"

"Aha, hanum, he—Ahmad Hadi Bey. He—the master's son—the Bey's son."

"Impossible! It is—not—"

"Aha, but yes, it is so. He—master's son."

Mute now, the white girl leant against the parapet.

"I have heard," the Turkish girl went on, "he

just returned. He been away—study—learn of the West world. Went away, hanum, when was—so high." The girl raised her hand to the height of her shoulder. "Master sent him—early—study. He been away—all long time. Now just come back—"

Daphnne leant against the parapet, letting the girl run on, scarcely hearing what she said.

With grey eyes that were almost black she looked down at the man in the garden. But no; there was no mistake. She knew that dark attractive face too well to be mistaken.

Pain, sharp, poignant, gripped her heart; pain that never before in all her sufferings had she felt.

He, the one man she had been unable to forget; he, who, with his youth and his ardent, virile life, had called to her in a way that had made her, involuntarily, respond—he was a Turk. He was the son of Ahmad Sueleman Bey!

Julian Conquest was the Turk's son!

She stumbled blindly from the terrace, sobbing, shedding passionate tears which in all her imprisonment in the Turkish palace she had not shed.

*   *   *

It was golden afternoon when Daphnne recovered from her paroxysm of grief.

Although she had called him a Turk, in her heart Daphnne had never for a moment believed Julian Conquest to be other than a white man.

She had, despite what she said, quite believed him to be Lieutenant Conquest—the Lieutenant Conquest whose place he evidently had taken.

But her words had been the truth. He was a

Turk—the son of a Turk! The revelation came as an absolute shock and brought a bitterness to her heart that was almost acute pain.

What fools they had been! she thought. Not only had they been deceived by the Turk but by the Turk's son. While the Bey had been deceiving them with false friendship, his son had been masquerading as one of them.

Could one wonder at this Turk's success! she thought with bitter rage. Could one wonder at his success with such a son! She felt she hated him for his beauty; hated him for his youth and attractiveness.

He was a Turk and he had attracted her in a way no white man had ever done!

With a swift, sudden movement she sprang up.

Her wild longing to escape was greater now than it had ever been before. She flashed a glance about the room from grey, shadowed eyes.

It was a lovely apartment, yet to her it was a gilded cage from which she could not escape. But even cages may lose a bar, and as she looked at the panel of the door she saw that it was slightly open.

The girls who attended her were in the bedchamber. Swiftly and cautiously Daphnne removed the bracelets from her arms and the anklets from her ankles and, moving softly across the floor, slipped out of the chamber.

She found herself in a kind of anteroom. In this room squatted a Turk.

White-faced, the girl shrank back. The native had his head back against the wall, his eyes closed, his mouth open.

From his hand dangled a pipe from which wavered up the faint fumes of hashish. Recovering herself, she started swiftly forward and sped soundlessly across the room to an openwork gateway which almost faced her.

For a moment this barrier stopped her. She was small and slim, however, and the Oriental clothes she wore, for all their elegance, were scanty.

Choosing a large opening in the gilded ironwork, she squeezed herself through with little difficulty. Down a wide passage beneath archways, through big chambers, small chambers, she went swiftly, soft-footed.

Coming out of one of the big apartments, she found herself on the balcony which ran along the back and both sides of the big palace hall.

Crouching by the balustrade, she looked down upon the wide, spacious, luxurious hall, yet the beauty was lost to her for she saw only the man who sat upon the big couch in the centre.

Slim and elegant in clinging silk, he lounged back on the cushioned seat.

Behind the couch a Turk stood motionless. Another moved about attentively with a tray. At the foot of the couch a native boy squatted, plucking the feathers of a fan.

Slowly Daphnne's glance travelled down the hall to the main entrance. Only the Turk's son and his attendants were between her and liberty.

Softly she moved round the balcony to the stairway at the back. The Turk's son sat up on his cushions and waved away his attendants with a petulant gesture.

Immediately they had gone, Ahmad Hadi

sprang up and walked swiftly across the floor. Parting the silken curtains at an entrance, he passed from sight.

Like an elusive spirit the girl came down the stairs, running lightly from pillar to pillar beneath the balcony. The curtains parted again and the son of the Turk stepped back into the hall. He moved forward a little way and then stopped short.

"Daphnne!" he gasped.

The girl stood rigid, regarding him across the hall. He moved swiftly to her.

"Daphnne!" he cried, and his hands went out to her in a swift, unconscious gesture.

But Daphnne shrank back against the pillar by which she stood. In the man's eager, thrilling voice, in the quick gesture of his hands, in the wild, glad light in his brown eyes, she saw only passion—desire; desire for herself!

She stared at the dark, youthful face she knew so well, saw the beauty of those golden eyes—yet, as she looked, she was aware of something that she had not noticed in the garden.

Those eyes were heavily darkened, and his face, too, was darker than when he had been with the English in far-away Trenedad.

"Daphnne!" he cried again, and took another step forward, a faltering, uncertain step.

"Daphnne—child—you are safe? The Turk—he—" He stopped, not because he could not find the words to go on with but because he could not say the words he wished to say.

Daphnne strove for a desperate moment to command her voice—to speak.

"Oh, yes," she gasped. "For all your scheming —I'm safe!"

The man drew a swift, short breath and steadied himself against one side of the couch, for so great was his relief. Only then, when he felt that relief, did he realise how much this woman meant to him.

"Oh, thank God!"

Even then, in that utterance, the woman could not hear the very heart of the man that spoke. She thought only that he was glad she had escaped the Turk—because he wanted her himself!

"Yes," her voice was low and hissing in tone, "for all your schemes and trickery, I'm safe!"

The man looked at her and caught his breath. The veil was but a screen of gauze and through it her slim body showed—the thin, clinging garments revealing every soft curve of her small, lissom form.

Her bare white flesh showed pale—soft. Against that whiteness was the gold of curling hair —the red of small, parted lips—

He felt suddenly the surge of warm, youthful blood; the longing of desires kept ruthlessly in check. The pulses throbbed a little heavily at his temples.

"Child!" he whispered, and passion and joy and wonder were mingled in his tone.

She leant against the pillar. The look in his eyes was such that a woman would be extremely happy to see in the eyes of a man. Yet anguish gripped her—anguish that was hardly endurable.

She knew that had he been the man she had always thought him to be, she would have been clasped in his arms at that moment—held fast against him.

All terror would have been of the past; she would have known security, protection.

But he was the Turk's son!

From her anguish anger arose, dominated her. She felt suddenly furious that he should see her so clad—should gaze upon her beauty.

"Don't come near me!" she gasped. "I hate you."

He stared a little then, with golden eyes that were wide and beautiful. The coldness of her reception of him was chilling the joy and the wonderful passion that rioted in him.

"You've no need to pose any more!" she cried. "Don't think you can go on deceiving us. I know you now—for what you are!"

"Daphnne—"

"You dare," she cried, "you dare to address me, to speak my name—you who are the Turk's son!"

He caught his breath slightly. He remembered. Yes, he had spoken her name, had all but betrayed himself. Who could say what listeners were about that hall, and in that palace many knew English.

"You've no need to try to deceive us any more," the girl went on in furious anger. "You see, I know you now. I know the way you've schemed and planned; I know the cunning way you deceived us!"

He drew back from her and slowly the look of gladness, of eager youth, faded from his golden eyes. Watching him, she saw the death of that ardent youth in his dark face—and crushed one end of her veil against her lips.

In some strange way it hurt her to see him

suffer. Yet, she told herself, she should be glad—glad! He was a Turk—the Bey's son!

"You shall pay for your work, though," she gasped. "You shall know that Englishmen won't allow the defiance and trickery of a Turk!"

Slowly he turned from her and the bitterness in his heart was greater than all the joy and tender passion that had been there before. This was his reception by the woman he had come to save; for whom he had dared so much.

This was her reception of him—he who, in that first meeting with the Bey, had faced the Turk with one hand hidden in the folds of his sash, grasping the butt of a revolver, since he had preferred death swift and sudden to any that an infuriated native might devise.

Yes, for her he had risked—worse than death, and—was she worth it?

He did not know that listening ears took an account of his meeting with the white girl to the Bey and that her attitude towards him saved him then.

From her position by the pillar the girl watched him as he stood, a slim, graceful figure by the big couch, and to her he seemed to be coolly indifferent or slightly mocking.

Anger rose in her. She left the pillar and approached the couch.

"You think that we are safely imprisoned in this palace here. But you'll find we're not so helpless. You'll find the English can act as well as you can scheme and plan. You think, perhaps because you're safe in your palace, under your father's care, that you are safe from the British, but you'll find you're mistaken."

The man stood rigid by the couch while the woman, quivering with fury, lashed him with her tongue—until he turned upon her with blazing golden eyes.

"Be quiet!"

She shrank a little then from his look.

"My God! Have you no faith—no trust?"

"No!" she cried. "We trust too often. We had faith when we believed you to be one of us and not a scheming Turk."

"Trust—no!" he cried. "You have none—none at all!"

Then he strove to master himself, to put a rein on the youthful passion which threatened for a moment to get utterly beyond his control.

"So—you think I'm the Turk's son?"

"Think?" she cried. "No. I know!"

He laughed and sank down upon the cushions of the couch.

"Do you know," he said, "for far less than what you have said to me the Turk's son would have that fair white flesh of yours quiver to the lash."

Her grey eyes dilated slightly; her small, slim hands tightened on the filmy veil, but she answered him with a stiffening of her slender figure.

"Oh, I daresay I know a little of Turks' ways now. You are used to lashing women, so it will be a change for you to fight a man, an Englishman!"

He laughed again, but his golden eyes held her grey ones. Through all the rage and bitterness that was surging in his heart he felt a little admiration. He found her undaunted, defiant, showing a spirit that aroused responsive admiration in him despite himself.

"You are a foolish child."

He took a cigarette from a box on a table by the couch and lit it without hurry.

"So foolish that it does not surprise me that you have found yourself in an Eastern harem!"

"We're here through the deceit and trickery of natives!"

"Not, of course, through your own foolishness?"

Daphnne gasped. Her grey eyes blazed at him with feminine fury.

"You have now seen another side of life. You have found you cannot rule Fate with your soft, wilful fingers, nor make everyone bend to your desires."

"I've found out the way of Turks," she gasped.

"You find yourself in a trap from which there is no escape."

"So you think!" she cried. "We shall escape—"

"Escape?"

He threw back his dark head and laughed, showing strikingly white teeth against his dark skin.

"Escape from here! If you can do that, I shall never think you as foolish as I do at the moment."

"You will find," she cried, "we can escape—"

"How? Tell me that. How can you escape from here?"

"Do you think I'd tell you?" she exclaimed.

Glittering grey eyes met gleaming brown. Bitterness and anger were in the hearts of both, for the want of understanding.

"You would be wise to do so," he said, "since you cannot get away from here without my help."

"Do you think I'd take help from you?"

With a swift, lithe movement he came up from the couch and his eyes blazed suddenly with passion.

She was caught in her first step of flight.

His arms were about her, he pulled her back against him, and his lips were on her mouth, hard, close, burning. She could not make the least effort of resistance. She was caught so suddenly, so swiftly. Before she realised his intention, she found herself crushed in his arms and his lips upon her own.

Then was she conscious of her own weakness —and his strength; a strength that amazed her, against which she could make no struggle, could not even move.

All the longing of a determinedly controlled life—the desire of a youthful, virile heart, the pent-up passion of many days—was in that kiss, and helpless she lay beneath the fire she had aroused.

Almost passively she rested in his arms. She felt robbed of all strength . . . half-fainting . . . yet with every sense quivering within her. . . .

Conscious only of his strong arms . . . his lips crushing hers with such force and passion . . .

When he released her, when his hold slightly relaxed, she did not for a moment move; then, exerting all her slight strength, she tore herself from him, panting.

The curtains at an entrance at the back of the hall were suddenly dragged apart and into the hall stepped two harem eunuchs.

Chapter Six

Daphnne Wayne paced from the terrace into the large room of the costly apartment in which she was confined, and back again to the terrace.

In the girl's heart was great unrest and the tumult of wild feelings. An utter restlessness had tortured her throughout the morning. Passionately she longed for freedom.

Wearied, she walked back to the big couch in the centre of the apartment and sat down upon the cushions.

Remembrance of what had happened the past afternoon held her. She had not been able to forget. Vivid in every detail, the scene in the hall came back to her. She thought of that meeting with him—the Turk's son—and that fierce, close kiss he had pressed upon her mouth—

Why hadn't she prevented it? she asked herself with sudden rage. Why hadn't she used her wits—done anything—to stop him mastering her, pressing that kiss upon her lips?

Why hadn't she screamed as she had when the Turk had held her in his arms? Yet, even as she knew that she had not felt the terror and repulsion in the arms of the son that she had felt in the arms of the Turk.

The wild passion of the younger man had thrilled her more than it had terrified her.

But she was furious that the son had triumphed over her even as the Turk seemed to be triumphing. Her glance wandered, fell upon the knife which lay on the small table by the couch.

She had been conscious enough to get it from the girdle of the big eunuch who had carried her back to her rooms from the palace hall.

As she regarded it she shuddered a little, wondering in what way she would have to use it.

A sound disturbed the still peace of the apartment. Rigidly the girl stiffened on the couch.

The sound of footsteps coming down the stone steps which led to the roof. The form of a man appeared upon the terrace.

It was the son of the Turk!

With a faint cry she sprang to her feet. Dragging a silken drapery from the couch about her bare white shoulders and breast, she went back a little.

"Daphnne—"

But the girl shrank away from him. A sudden fear seized her; she felt the heavy throb of a pulse in her throat. Looking at him, she realised, that he was the Turk's son. That, here, he could do just as he pleased, could have whatever he desired—and he had come to her!

The man stopped in the room between the terrace and the couch. His expression changed.

"So," he said, and it seemed he guessed her thoughts, "you realise our positions now. You

realise that they have—altered. You could do as
you pleased, you could say what you liked—before; but now it is I who may speak as I wish, and
have whatever I want—"

He laughed a little, looking upon her shrinking form.

"You realise that?"

"Why . . . have you come here?" she gasped.

"Perhaps to find you," he answered.

He looked at her. He had fulfilled his desire;
he had held her helpless in his arms—had kissed
her small, red lips. Yet he was aware that he still
desired to hold her—to feel her lips beneath his
own.

"I have come to know whether you will now
accept my help."

She recovered a little; fear lessened. She could
not forget his quick capture of her—his sudden
burning kiss. She felt she hated him for making it
so.

"No, I will not!" she cried.

He sank upon the big couch on which she
had been sitting.

"Yet," he said, "you cannot get away from
here unless you let me help you."

She regarded him; gazed at the darkly handsome face she knew so well. She took a step forward, nearer to him. Anger was swiftly stirring in
her, overmastering all fear.

"So you may think!" she cried. "But you may
find it otherwise!"

"No; I know." He shook his head.

"You think you have me, an Englishwoman,
safely imprisoned here," she exclaimed, her lovely

figure in the shielding silk trembling a little, for his indolent attitude on the couch increased her anger.

"But the English will find out. They'll come and you'll suffer for this! I shall escape—"

"I don't think so. If you will not take the only chance—let me help you—must I think you prefer to stay here? Come here."

She did not stir. Yet she was acutely conscious that he had but to summon attendants to have his will obeyed, or to rise from the couch to have her in his arms.

He moved slightly and immediately, with an action uncontrollable; she bent to the knife on the small table by the couch, but even as her fingers touched it his hand was about her wrist.

Fiercely she strove for possession of the knife. He dragged her onto the couch with him and for a moment they struggled amidst the gorgeous cushion.

Then he had got it from her hand and flung it across the room to the terrace. He laughed a little.

"So—you can fight! I had never thought you capable of it—soft, pampered, civilised child. It's pleasant to know you're a woman to this extent. But it's useless, Daphnne. It's useless—here—against me. You believe—"

He stopped as, with fresh fury, she struggled again in his hold, but her efforts did not make him release her; instead his arms tightened about her and he crushed her against him amidst the disordered cushions.

"You must know that you cannot have everything as you desire. You will not realise that life is not so much taking, but giving. But you shall give to me. Your kisses—"

Deliberately he bent and pressed his mouth upon hers. With wild fury she strove still to struggle, but his strong arms about her made all efforts of resistance futile.

As before, she realised herself powerless—crushed in his arms. She could feel the fire of his youthful blood and the heavy beating of his heart upon her own.

"You have never suffered—you do not know what pain is," he said, and crushed her a little more deliberately against him.

Yet the pain he caused her slender body, the way he hurt her lips, seemed nothing to the anguish of her soul.

"You shall have the kisses of the Turk's son," he said, and pressed his lips swiftly and with the warmth of passion upon her cheeks and mouth and bare white throat.

His kisses seemed to drug her . . . to hold her captive to his will. . . . His touch, his strength, seemed to take all power of resistance from her. . . . She felt herself yielding . . . responding. . . .

Unresisting she lay upon the cushions, and he was caressing her—caressing her bare shoulders, her arms, her slender form. . . .

She drew an unsteady breath, feeling a deeper anguish which overmastered anger and sweet ecstasy.

His lips claimed hers again; his hand lay against her breasts. . . .

The afternoon dragged in languid, fragrant, golden minutes. . . . Faintly through the languorous silence there came a sound—soft footsteps, light voices.

The man heard, withdrew his arms from about the girl, and rose from the couch.

Beyond the silken curtains, in the bedchamber, women's voices spoke lightly. He turned and walked across the floor to the terrace.

When the Turkish girls, her attendants, entered the big apartment, the son of the Turk had gone.

* * *

Daphnne Wayne sat in the big chamber of her luxurious apartment, paying no attention to the luscious fruits, rich sweetmeats, costly jewels, and garments—which were brought to her by her attendants.

Weary dragging hours went by and the Turk made no move, gave no sign. The suspense was almost unendurable.

She almost welcomed the intense emotions, the longings and desires, stirred within her by the Turk's son, since they kept her a little from thinking of the loathed Bey.

Hope was almost dead.

It seemed that she could not escape the Turk. Or, if not the Turk, there was the Turk's attractive son. That son who could, without doubt, have everything that he wanted from his father!

Slowly the dusk of the evening deepened, darkened the chamber.

In the darkness the Turkish girls closed the shutters and lit lamps.

The night advanced. Its advance brought

sickening dread to the white girl. The darkness seemed menacing. Then the panel of the door swung open and into the apartment stepped two big eunuchs.

With a gasping catch of breath the white girl came to her feet and swayed a little.

The men ordered her to come with them. Chill terror held the girl's heart. She thought of refusing and then saw the utter uselessness of it.

Down passages and out to the balcony that overlooked the palace hall they took her. Then down the wide staircase at the back.

As she reached the foot of the stairs the white girl stopped—stood, amazed—fascinated by the scene in the hall before her.

In the centre of the hall, on the shining, tessellated floor, almost in a circle had been placed cushions and rugs of various patterns and brilliance.

Sitting cross-legged at the head of the circle was Sueleman Bey, a gorgeous figure in a green robe embroidered with pearls.

On his left, his son, wearing a yellow robe girdled with a red sash. About him in elegant robes and wearing jewels stood a number of his Turks.

Glaring light was thrown upon the scene by a number of hanging lamps and in this jewels flashed, silken robes shimmered. With a hand pressed to her heart, the girl stood, moving only when the eunuchs drew her forward before the Turk.

Terror and loathing—an instinctive loathing for some assurance, clenching her hands to keep from betraying the shiver that shook her.

The son of the Turk appeared utterly indifferent, almost unconscious of the white girl's presence.

"O fair white pearl in the Orient." Sueleman Bey's voice came softly—caressingly. "Will you not be wise? Will you not give to me the answer that is my desire?"

"No!" gasped the white girl, forcing herself to speak, dreading another exhausting battle of words.

Baffled desire, rage, changed the Turk's face; his dark hands clenched.

"You shall be given no more mercy!" His voice changed. "You shall know I will not be defied! For this have I sent for you. Sufficiently long have you been within my palace—attended upon. Now —this night—"

She pressed her hand to her heart, which seemed to throb with a heaviness that exhausted.

"The decision shall be made. You shall decide. That privilege do I grant to you."

Sueleman Bey rose from his cushions, stood a tall, dark, powerful figure upon his feet, and almost instinctively the girl shrank a little. The Turk's son rose also, coming lithely to his feet.

"You shall decide," snarled Sueleman Bey. "Listen. You are a woman for whom the hearts of men crave with fierce desire. I desired you—but I want not resistance. My son, who knows the ways of white women, has feelings different. He has looked upon your beauty, and desire for you has flamed within his heart. My son desires you!"

Daphnne gasped. With a swift, almost wild action she turned and, with dark, dilated eyes, looked at the son of the Turk.

But Ahmad Hadi, the Turk's son, stood without looking at her. His handsome dark face was inscrutable.

"My son is the light of my heart. There is little that I can refuse him," came the Turk's voice. "And he desires—you."

She felt a tumult of emotions which, allied to her terror, almost overpowered her. But the throb of her heart was wild. . . .

Then, after what seemed an age of time, she heard again the voice of the Turk. Wildly she struggled to control herself.

"Because you are a white woman and privileged beyond other women, you shall choose between us. You shall choose—to which one of us you will belong!"

Her hand still against her bare white throat, she drew a gasping breath. So it was to be a choice—a choice—the Turk's son or the Turk?

"You hear? Choose now! And I will give my orders for you!"

"No, no!" she gasped, dragging her look from the son's regard. "I will not choose! I'll choose neither of you!"

"Then," said the Turk, "you shall be given to my men!"

A gasping cry came from the girl's lips. She could not even look round at the waiting forms of the Turks.

"They hope very much you will not choose! They have rarely seen such white beauty as you possess. A skin the hue of milk—a soft body of curving shape—that would light desire in a man's breast with the flame of fire—"

She cried out again, stopping him.

The son of the Turk stood without a movement, his dark, youthful face unstirred, but the jewels on his breast gleamed as they rose and fell.

"Choose!" cried Sueleman Bey.

Wildly, with grey eyes dark and wide, Daphnne looked about her. Yet she knew there was no way of escape—no help. She was trapped.

She would have to give herself to one of them! Be the possession of a Turk! His toy—his pleasure for the space of an hour—

She swayed a little, and then, aware of the glaring, voluptuous scene surrounding her, strove wildly to keep consciousness.

She, the lovely, popular Colonel's daughter, who would give herself to no man whatever he had offered her—now, to be the plaything of a Turk!

And she could not even have the release of death, since nowhere could death be found. There was no escape—no help.

The Turk—?

Or the Turk's son—?

"Choose!" cried Sueleman Bey. "To whom will you give your rare white beauty? The dark, scented hours of this waiting night are passing! Choose!"

But with a hand pressed to her throbbing pulses the white girl shrank back. Terror held her, deepened, seemed to crush her heart with icy, merciless fingers.

The Turk approached her, full lips parted, black eyes gleaming, a hand held out—

Terror reached the height of endurance.

She moved by impulse—acted instinctively. Turning, with a gasping breath, she fled to the arms of the Turk's son.

In the silence that held for a moment in the

great hall, a distant tom-tom was heard throbbing
faintly.

The woman, half-fainting in the arms of the
Turk's son, was hardly conscious of that silence.
Her senses were deadened.

She felt that in the arms of the younger man
the Turk could not touch her. She scarcely realised
that she had given herself bodily to the Turk's son.

What her action would mean to her she did
not at first realise. She knew only that she had
acted on ungovernable impulse. She had had no
will in the matter; blindly she had fled to that
one man.

As his arms had closed about her, holding her
limp form to him, she had heard him draw a swift
breath and was vaguely aware that, as well as
for relief, it could stand for triumph.

Then an ejaculation of rage from the Turk
broke the silence in the hall.

Fury showed in Sueleman Bey's black eyes;
his hands clawed the air. Almost ungovernable
rage surged in him for a moment.

The eyes of father and son met and held. In
the golden eyes of the younger man was a merciless determination—a narrowed look that amazed,
startled the Bey.

Almost unconscious as she was, the girl saw
him slip his other hand beneath the folds of his
sash and instinct told her he had a revolver.

Wonder stirred in her. Was he determined to
fight for her in that way—against his father? Did
he desire her to that extent?

Tension was still stiff in the hall; but through
it was an undercurrent of unrest—the surge of un-
restrained, primitive passions.

"The white woman has chosen, O my father," said the son of the Turk.

Sueleman Bey remained looking at his son, but the gaze of the younger man held steady on his.

Then, slowly, the Turk's look altered a little. The tenseness went out of his big form.

In his black eyes hate and malice showed, and in place of baffled desire came an expression of cruel pleasure.

"Aye, take her!" he almost hissed. "Make her suffer. Make her your slave, Ahmad my son. Make her soft, white body writhe in your hands."

Hearing, the woman realised her position and shivered, and the man who held her felt the shuddering of her lightly clad body in his arms.

"You do understand, Ahmad?" hissed the Bey. "Make her know you are her master and she but your slave to be treated as it is your pleasure. You do understand?"

"I understand," returned the Turk's son, and his voice was now cool and hard.

"Go, then," hissed the Turk. "Go. Take her!"

Swiftly the Turk's son bent and lifted the shivering, half-clad form of the woman easily in his arms.

Turning, without another word, he carried her from the hall.

Through the close atmosphere of luxurious chambers, through the dusk of passages, and beneath the light of lamps, the son of the Turk carried the woman, bearing her small, light form with ease.

Pushing through heavy curtains, he stopped for a moment and the warm, scented air told the woman he had entered an apartment. She opened weary, almost black eyes.

It was a luxurious chamber. At one end, across the apartment from wall to wall, hung heavy silken curtains, a dark golden colour in the subdued light.

Behind the man the entrance curtain swayed together, heavy and impenetrable as any closed door. Leisurely he walked across the apartment, moving towards the wide, golden curtains.

The woman in his arms shivered and he felt again the trembling of her small, supple body; felt too the beating of her heart.

Parting those thick silken curtains, he passed through them into an inner chamber—a room of Eastern splendor. A single lamp was burning but with only sufficient light to show the big, low Eastern bed. Curtains hung on every side, seeming to enclose the chamber.

Instinctively—in the voluptuous atmosphere of that room, of faint gold light and dark shadow, of silence and clinging warmth—he held her soft, slim body closer in his arms.

The woman stirred a little but did not open her eyes and her lashes lay heavy and dark on her pale cheeks. Terror and horror had been left in the hall; only fear and a strange, wild feeling, which made her heart throb in her throat, remained.

The atmosphere of the room was like a drug to her. . . . He, with his ardent youth and perfect health, would have to exert his strength so little to have her helpless. . . .

Walking across to the wide, luxurious bed, he placed her upon the cushions and she sank into their yielding softness. His strong, slender fingers slipped about her throat. He found the clasps of the strings of pearls and one after another drew them from about her neck.

Then he loosened the band which confined the diaphanous veil and drew band and veil from her head, leaving her short gold curls free.

Still she did not resist, nor even move. Only her breast heaved beneath the small, clinging jacket and a pulse throbbed in her bare throat.

Yet every sense, every nerve, was on the alert. Lying passive on the cushions, she strove to collect every particle of her remaining strength for the struggle that she felt must come.

Yet the very thought of resistance seemed to take all power from her. The hot, sensuous air of that dusky apartment seemed to rob her of the little remaining strength she had.

Her half-clad limbs seemed chained to the gorgeous cushions; she felt unable even to raise her head. Against his strength and virile life she felt quite helpless—incapable even of fighting.

With a strong, caressing hand he pushed the damp gold curls back from her forehead.

As she lay on the cushions every soft curve of her body seemed to show with arresting loveliness. He felt the blood hot as fire at his temples.

Abruptly he rose from the bed and walked to where a curtain was looped back, revealing another entrance to the apartment. Dragging the curtain down, he closed the entrance.

As he turned back to her, the girl dragged her small, light-clad form up upon the cushions.

"No—no!" Her words came but faintly. "Oh, please—please be merciful! Don't—"

He stood and looked down at her, but a yard from the bed. Her fair beauty was arresting against the brilliant cushions. The lamplight gleamed upon her golden hair and white shoulders. . . .

They were far from civilisation—and the night was lovely—and she was his. . . .

Why could he not forget! Why could he not keep master of himself; crushed under his habitual cool hardness the passionate youth in him that clamoured for recognition!

He moved a step over the soft carpets.

"Please—please!" Her low voice was almost inarticulate. "Don't—"

He stood looking at her. Then he went to the golden curtains, passed through them, and flung them together behind him.

Going swiftly across the chamber, he dragged back curtains which had hidden an open, jasmine-hung terrace and stepped out into white moonlight.

The strain of that night had been so great; he had not thought that he had yet more to go through—a strife with himself.

The youthful, virile life in him, over which in the past he had kept firm control, clamoured now to be recognised—to be acknowledged and satisfied.

Longings and desires long suppressed rose now and would not be denied. Why should he spare her? he asked himself. From the very first she had treated him with scorn, with mockery.

Why should he spare her now that she was his?

He had done a daring thing, had risked worse

than death for her sake—and she had repaid him with scorn, with words of hate and fury.

If he had to suffer for her—why should he not take some reward now? The man drew a heavy breath and stood with slender hands clenched at his sides.

He wanted her—and she was his for the taking! Dear God, how hard it was!

She expected no mercy from him—though the Turk had sent her to his arms.

Why, then, should he consider her? Why should he show her mercy? Through her the lives of many Englishmen had been imperilled. She was a lovely pampered child who would take everything from life and give nothing. Unless—

Wildly he checked his thoughts and forced himself to concentrate on the terrace. The night was beautiful—and the beauty of it seemed to take him by the throat.

Stillness enveloped the palace. The quietness was intense—expectant.

Perhaps never again would she be his as she was his this night.

In that Turkish palace she belonged to him. There the laws of civilisation did not count. They were in the East now—and the East had given her to him!

Why, then, did he hesitate?

He had given so much in life and had taken little. He had worked hard—for others—and had taken no reward for himself.

Why did he not take for all he had given? Why did he not take repayment now? This night was his—offering him reward—

He stepped back from the scented moonlight, clung to the curtains that had veiled the terrace.

There was the chance that they would never get away from that palace. The probability was that they would not both escape alive. But they had this night. This night was theirs. . . .

He gripped the silken hangings. He felt utterly weary; but the strong, virile life in him would not let him rest. Her beauty was before him in the dusk . . . the feel of her body in his arms . . . her hair against his lips. . . .

With fierce desperation he clung to the soft folds of the terrace curtains. All the wild, eager life in him urged him to that inner room, but he clung to the curtains, clung as if, by exerting physical strength, he would hold himself back.

He prayed for the dawn—prayed desperately, passionately. If only it would come quickly—if only it would come—quickly—

Chapter Seven

The palace of the Turk basked in golden sunlight, fanned by light summer breezes.

Towards the end of a still, close afternoon, in the apartment of the Turk's son, Daphnne Wayne sat on a cushioned seat facing the open terrace.

The white veil had slipped off one shoulder; the small, pearl-encrusted jacket clinging so closely to her breast, a part of the bare waist below, so slender and exquisitely white, the jeweled girdle of silk drawers encircling curving hips.

Clasping her hands tightly about her silk-clad knees, she looked out beyond the terrace. Everything seemed different after that night—that unforgettable night. The whole world seemed, in some way, to have changed.

She could scarcely realise that that night was past; that, safely, she had come through it. Wonder held her; wonder that had remained with her through the days and nights that had followed that unforgettable night.

She had been spared—the man to whom she had been given had spared her! If before she had not been able to understand the nature of this man, she knew it now. He had been revealed to her in a way that left her mute with wonder.

The strength and the fineness of him were revealed to her. The more she thought of that night, the more did she marvel at the strength of him that had made forbearance possible.

She knew how great had been his desire. She had felt his passion—a passion that had thrilled her at the same time that it made her fear—and yet he had been able to leave her.

She had shown him no kindness. From their very first meeting she had shown hostility towards him—had flung him scornful, derisive words, and yet, when he had been able to take repayment from her, he had been merciful to her.

He had got her for himself from the Bey, and yet he himself had not harmed her. That night she had looked for no mercy, even from him, but he had shown her how unworthy was her fear.

She had been his—for the taking—and he had spared her. Down in her heart Daphnne knew, with a woman's knowledge, what it had cost him to give her up that night.

Daphnne, for the first time in her life, knew a depth of gratitude—a gratitude that hurt with its intensity.

She no longer hated him, no longer loathed him as she had said. He had made hate and loathing utterly impossible. Instinct had been right; instinct had not erred in sending her to his arms.

For twenty-four hours, after that night, she had been quite undisturbed, but at the end of that time the Turk's son had made her acutely aware that she was living in those rooms with him.

She did not, however, meet him in that inner, curtained room.

On the second day she had come upon him in the big main apartment and he had caught her in his arms and kissed her—a long fierce kiss that had told her something of the hunger of his heart.

And she had rested in his arms unresisting. After that night—his strength—she had been utterly unable to feel any anger. He had taken all resentment from her by what he had done. She had lain in his arms and had returned his kiss!

She did not know if she was a prisoner in his rooms. On the second day she had ventured out of the big apartment and through another entrance —into a room which held various masculine attire and a neat young Turk.

Swiftly she had returned to the double apartment and since then had made no further attempt to find the main entrance.

As yet she had not been able to think of any plans for altering her position or for helping her father and friends who were prisoners in that palace, perhaps through her own foolishness.

Her eyes closed completely. The atmosphere of the big apartment in that quiet hour of late afternoon was soothing.

With a startling suddenness and an unexpectedness that was disconcerting, the heavy curtains at the entrance were parted and Ahmad Hadi stepped between them, into the apartment.

The man walked to the terrace, to where the slim, fair girl sat so stiffly on the cushioned seat.

Sinking to one knee on the cushions, he put out a hand, touched her hair—slipped his fingers through her short gold curls—caressingly.

111

Daphnne did not stir, made no movement of withdrawal, but her slim, light-clad form was stiff on the cushions.

"My fair little slave!" he said softly.

She put one hand to her throat. He rose from the cushions, slim and lithe by the couch.

"Is it not an unbearable thought—that you belong now to that hated son of the Turk?"

The sun, a blaze of gold, was nearing the western horizon. The sky in the east changed from darkest blue to deep purple.

The man moved from the table, went out to the terrace. Standing there at his ease, he regarded the sunset, looked down upon the palace garden.

Cautiously, feeling still the throb of pulses under her hand, the girl raised her eyes to regard him through dark lashes.

Against the pillar he was clearly outlined to Daphnne by the purple-tinted sky. A youthful, graceful outline which yet showed supple strength.

She caught her lower lip between her teeth, feeling again a searing pain in her heart. If only she knew! If only she could understand—

In a blaze of gold and crimson the sun had set. About the garden, faint misty dusk was stealing. Yet still the man remained upon the terrace while the sky swiftly darkened.

In a little while the moon rose and sent pale radiance to lighten the night's darkness.

"Daphnne."

She started upon the cushions as she heard her name, though he spoke it in the way he usually did, dragging it to full length.

"Daphnne—come here and see how beautiful the night is."

Her wide grey eyes regarded him but he leant still against the pillar. She did not move. He turned then, looked at her, and moving his arm held it out to her with a quick gesture of invitation.

She caught her breath and turned her head quickly, for that eager, persuasive gesture of his arm held out to her was cruelly irresistible.

He laughed softly; then, with a sudden swift movement, he took a step from the terrace, caught her hand, and pulled her up from the cushions.

Laughing still, he slipped his arm about her and held her to him.

"Don't you want to come to me? Don't you want to see the beauty of what the world holds?"

She rested heavily against him, making not the least resistance, though her slender figure trembled to the touch of his arm round her bare waist.

He glanced down at her and she was aware of his dark face; yet, for all that, it was the strong, attractive face she always wished to look upon.

"Look at the sky, child. It's night's velvet cloak now. And the stars are diamonds upon the velvet. Don't you see?"

It was a still, close night. The air was warm and subtly scented. Nothing moved within the gardens.

"Look, child, the moon's up. Do you know it's the night's lamp? Soon it'll flood the land with silver light."

She strove desperately for speech. She felt she must say something, answer him.

"Yes," she gasped out, "there's beauty here—but in it there's horror—awful things—"

"I know," he said, without the least change of

tone. "But that horror comes only from the hearts of men, which are sometimes vile. Not from Nature does it come. Nature is ever beautiful—ever wonderful."

Daphnne felt that she was answered, and drooped a small, mute figure against him while the heavy jasmine scent rose and surrounded them.

"Does the night tell you nothing, Daphnne? Do you read nothing of its meaning, or feel—?"

She stiffened, grey eyes wide and dark.

"Do you know that at night the fountains cease to play?"

She strained against his encircling arm.

"Do you know that the lily only shows its glory to the night? That its virgin whiteness blushes rosy with the dusky hours—"

She tore herself from him and fled back into the chamber. With wildly throbbing pulses she lay upon the cushions. It was madness, she told herself. Madness to care, to be so disturbed—

She should hate him.

Yet she found herself desiring only to be with him—longing to hear his voice telling her of the beauty of the world that before she had scarcely noticed—delighting in the touch of his hands and lips—

It was madness!

He stood awhile upon the terrace and then stepped into the chamber. He came to her through the dusk and sank down upon the couch.

Bending slowly forward, he pressed his lips against the bare white shoulder turned to him. His lips were warm against her flesh. Daphnne closed her eyes; clenched small hands in the cushions.

She longed for him to go, leave her—then, as ardently, desired him to stay. The caress of his lips hurt—yet was so sweet.

"Why won't you listen to me when I would tell you of the beauty of life, Daphnne? Why won't you let me show you what life can be?"

His hands closed about her arms, slipped down their bare softness with a touch that was caressing—yet still she could find no anger, could not resist him.

She felt that, if he wished, this one man could win her, even against her will! If he desired, he could have her willing—and not unwilling—

"It was such a cold, unfeeling little heart," he said, resting one hand against her bare side. "Yet I thought it could be so different—and so I spared it. I spared it—though it was so hard to do so."

She drew a quick breath, but lay still mute on the cushions.

He slipped his arms about her, drew her out of their softness, close against his strong, slim body. Her hands pressed against his breast. She shivered with the longing that seemed to drag her heart from her.

The virile life of him seemed to claim her. It was cruelly hard to resist, to fight herself.

"Hasn't it been touched yet—that heart of yours? Doesn't it seek and long or know the deep, wild feelings of life?" He tried to see into her averted eyes as she lay now within his arms.

Failing, he pressed her back a little into the cushions and kissed her throat—felt all the warm, responsive life of her under his lips.

"Daphnne, don't you understand now? Or is it that you won't yield—won't give me one kind

115

word? Do you know what love can be—you who play with it? I wonder if you could feel love in all its strength! Love with passion—with rapture and longing!"

Her breath came swiftly; her eyes were suddenly tight-closed.

"Can you tell me you don't know—? In my arms you say you don't know the desire of life— the longing of love? With my heart beating upon yours, can you tell me that you have no answer for me—that you don't care?"

Her hand went up to his shoulder; her small, white fingers slowly clenched in the velvet of his jacket.

Feeling her hold upon him, the tightening clasp of her slender fingers, he laughed softly but with a note of tenderness. He bent to her, and his warm breath came upon her lips.

"Daphnne—you care!"

But her small trembling lips would give him no answer, no words.

"Child, in love there's wonder and glory—"

Her grey eyes slowly unclosed.

"Wonder and glory," he whispered, "and because of that I spared you."

He looked down at her pale, lovely face against his shoulder, into her half-veiled eyes. All that lips would not speak, eyes betrayed.

Yet the woman strove not to yield.

She longed to surrender—to cling to him with all the passion that was now in her heart; yet she fought that longing, strove desperately not to respond.

"I love you," he whispered swiftly, bending

116

to her till her lips were beneath his. "Daphnne—my woman."

Her hand went about his neck, her arms clung about him even as his crushed her to him. She raised her head a little; their lips met and clung.

It was inevitable—that kiss. A kiss that had all the ardour of pure passion, the tenderness of love. A kiss that demanded and surrendered, that claimed and gave.

Love laughed triumphant.

Time dragged in magic, blissful moments—moments in which all thought of the world was lost. After a while, however, she, the woman, was conscious of a vague unrest which forced itself in upon the sweet madness that possessed them; was aware that it was not right.

His arms tightened yet more about her and then she got a little weak strength to resist.

"No—no!" she gasped.

A little wildly she struggled out of his arms.

"Oh, have you forgotten we're here?" she gasped still, panting a little, facing him with tragic grey eyes and fair face white in the moonlight. "How can you speak of love? Have you forgotten—we're here—in this vile Turk's palace?"

The man rose slowly to his feet. The youth and eagerness died from his face and the lines came again.

"I'd forgotten." His voice was level.

Turning abruptly, before she even guessed his intention, he moved from the couch, went swiftly across the rugs to the entrance.

The heavy curtains, dragged apart by his slim

117

hands, were flung together behind him. Silence fell upon the apartment.

"Julian!" her cry went out to him.

Then she crushed one small hand against her lips. Was it—Ahmad?

A slim, limp form, she sank into the disordered cushions of the soft couch.

* * *

Ahmad Sueleman Bey softly approached the costly apartment of his son. Soundlessly he walked across a passage, parted silken curtains, and stepped within.

Inside was the white woman, standing with hands clasped before her, her gold curls a bright mass about her head.

"Aha," murmured the Turk.

Swiftly she looked up, saw him, and her grey eyes dilated. In the dusk of the room, which was only half-lighted by the pale glow of sunset without, the Bey seemed to loom a muscular, gigantic figure.

The dread, the loathing, which she had always felt before in his presence in that palace, seemed to take her by the throat.

She could not move, could not take a step away; for the moment she felt paralysed.

His dark, hawk-like features showed in the gloom beneath a crimson, tasselled cap. She saw his eyes, the curve of his cruel yet sensual lips— saw the passion and desire that leapt into his look at the sight of her.

He put out a dark hand and touched her

118

shoulder—then it seemed the spell broke. The touch of his fingers on her flesh brought her suddenly to quivering, shuddering life.

With a half-choked cry she started away, reeled back from him; then, turning, she fled across the floor to heavy curtains on one side, and was gone from sight.

The Turk, with barely a pause, started swifty after her, across the floor to the curtains.

However, before he could reach them, Ahmad Hadi stepped into the chamber and sprang between the Bey and those heavy curtains which swayed still in the shadow.

With a soft ejaculation the Bey stopped short. His brilliant black eyes flashed at his son who had sprung in front of him.

Neither spoke for the moment; neither moved. The tension in the antechamber was stiff for a few palpitating seconds. On the other side of the curtains, clinging to them with one hand, shivering, stood the girl, scarcely daring to breathe.

The mad rage, coming, a good deal, from thwarted desire, which had leapt up within the Turk, slowly cooled down.

The Bey thought he could understand. His son's action had been unmistakable. Sueleman Bey was very much the Oriental. The most important of his feminine possessions were kept in rigid Oriental seclusion.

And his son was but regarding those laws. This woman had been given to him and his action had been to show plainly that she was utterly his possession.

The Turk stepped back a pace. He desired the

woman—yes—but against him there were those rigid laws which he, himself, so relentlessly enforced.

He craved for possession of her, but could he disregard those laws? Could he take her from the arms of his son, to whom he had given her?

"Ahmad," his voice came softly, "have you not tired of her? She is a cold pale woman but the delight of a few days. Have you not yet tired of her?"

Just the other side of the curtains, Daphnne caught a small hand to her parted lips.

"No, my father," Ahmad Hadi's answer came cold and emotionless, "I have not yet tired of her."

"It is now surely time—let her be given to my men who burn now with impatience—"

"My father," came the son's cold voice, "I have not yet tired of this woman."

The Turk's dark hands plucked at the silken robe he wore; then he turned slowly and stepped out of the chamber. The thick curtains were parted, and the girl swayed between them, into the arms of the man who had stood in front of them.

Her weight was heavy against him; her small hands clung to him.

"You won't let him have me—you won't let him take me!" she panted.

She clung to him, conscious only of the wild desire to cling to a strength she felt could save her, and the strong, lithe form of him was strangely sweet, wonderfully soothing to her terror.

With scarcely an effort he held her, his supple muscles supporting her dead weight almost with ease.

"Did you think I would, Daphnne? Did you think that possible? Did you think I'd give you up?"

With masculine force his arms tightened about her so that she lay against him, crushed to him.

"Did you think that? He shall never have you!"

Her fear lessened; slowly the awful dread which had made her shiver in the warm, close dusk left her. In his arms she could not fear; feeling his strength, she was aware of a sense of security; the fierce hold of his arms about her was sweet.

Swiftly the dusk of evening deepened.

The man went to a big couch in the centre of the chamber and sank down upon it, holding the girl still in his arms. Her small hands still clung to him, keeping him; for the night's darkness in the room brought back a little of her dread.

He had been the only one to give her help. In that Turkish palace he had been the only man who had stood between her and awful peril.

She clung to this one man now for protection, hardly aware that she did so. So—yet again—she found herself resting in the arms of the Turk's son on silken cushions.

Her slight form trembled a little as he stroked the gold disordered curls that lay against his shoulder.

In a little while she fell asleep in his arms.

For a time the chamber was enveloped in shadow and then it was illuminated by the moon. The man looked down at the woman who slept in his arms. Unchecked, he gazed at the sweet beauty of her, just discernible in the light of the moon.

Tight-closed eyes had circles of shadow beneath; small curved lips were parted a little. Her curls against his shoulder were all disordered; her bare white breast heaved above the tight, pearl-stiffened bodice with the unrest of her breath....

She was in his arms now—the woman who had kept sleep from him in the nights that had followed their meeting in the faraway civilised world of theirs.

Warm and heavy she lay on his heart; the silk of her hair was against his lips....

Yet she was not his.

All the loveliness he hungered for was in his arms—yet his hand that was across her gripped the butt of his revolver. Still the woman slept—and the man watched.

Nothing, however, disturbed the still peace of the night. No sign of lurking peril came in the dark, quiet moments.

Through the long, mystic hours the man did not relax his vigil. His fingers grew cold about the revolver he held. And still the woman slept in his arms.

The pale light of dawn was stealing into the room when Daphnne awoke. Slipping from the man's arms, she slid off the couch and stood up.

Standing motionless in the half-light of that strange hour, she presseed a hand to her cheek. Realisation came to her that she had slept all night in the arms of this man!

She looked down at him. He was sleeping

then. And it was a haggard young face she saw in the eerie light of dawn.

She noticed the marring lines about the dark-lashed eyes and the even mouth; signs which spoke of sleeplessness, days of strain. Faintly she realised how much he had done; what he was giving—

A strange, new tenderness surged up in her. Her eyes, gazing upon him, had, of a sudden, all the soft, wonderful look of a woman's eyes.

Slowly she bent till her lips rested against his dark cheek. Yet, so softly did she touch him that he, drugged by weariness, did not awaken.

If he dreamt she kissed him, what was there to tell him it was not all dream but reality when he awoke?

* * *

It was a little after noon when Ahmad Hadi returned to the apartment.

Daphnne rose to her feet. A strip of pink silk was across her slight form. There was deep colour in her cheeks but her delicate face was calm.

The man stopped by the ottoman. In one hand he held white draperies.

"Daphnne, I hope you're ready to help me." He spoke abruptly and his voice came cold and hard.

"Tonight—or rather it will be tomorrow—the attempt to get away from here will be made. You'll realise it's not been an easy thing for me to do—to plan your freedom and that of Wayne and the others. But I've managed it at last. You've got to get away tonight. Be ready—"

Slowly Daphnne turned.

He was wearing riding-dress: a long grey coat of Eastern cut, light breeches, and riding-boots with spurs. He looked different, more English, far less Oriental.

His face was hard. Staring at the dark, good-looking countenance, she sought in vain for the haggard young face of the dawn.

His face now was stiffly set, his even mouth had the old hardness, and his golden, darkened eyes were cold with their look of determination.

In vain she looked for the tender guardian of the past night. He stood now in the costly, voluptuous room, stiff, formidable—half-arrogant.

"These things"—he dropped the white clothes he held upon the ottoman without looking at her—"are trousers and a jacket I've got from Selim, my young attendant. You must put them on—over that dress you're wearing. There'll be riding to do—hard riding—if we get away, as we must!"

Still Daphnne's mind was blank to all but one thought. The thought that he was helping them to escape; that he had been planning to save them from the Turk!

Over and over it repeated itself. He was planning their freedom—had been, all the time, working to get them from the Bey!

"Be ready for me when I come to you to-night. It won't be much before dawn. And send the women away."

He stopped. His slim, lithe figure was rigidly straight—strangely tense.

"I've planned the attempt for an hour or two before dawn. Then, if at any time, the palace is likely to be quiet. You and your father must be

124

away from the palace, and the province if possible, before daylight."

The girl was conscious of a wild desire to speak. There was so much she wanted to say—so much to say—to tell him. Yet she felt unable to say a word; incapable of speaking. Mute she stood before him.

In that moment she did not think of the attempt to escape—but only of the man who had planned it. Her thoughts of him were all confused. She did not understand. She was conscious of no wild elation at the thought of freedom—only a vague relief that the situation was to end.

"I'll keep my attendants away from the rooms and you must get rid of the women. The Bey must get no breath of suspicion. My God, so much depends now— You understand, Daphnne?"

She spoke then. Words sprang from her lips, swiftly, impulsively, almost against her will.

"You are coming with us?"

The man turned from her, took a step towards the centre couch. The merciless control he was keeping on himself nearly went then.

His hands clenched at his sides and he fought for command; fought ardent nerves and youthful muscles that rebelled against his unyielding will, rebelled for life.

"If I can," he answered, and his voice was hard and cold.

"Oh, you must! You must! I—" Wildly she burst out then, and then checked—crushed one small hand against her parted lips.

Although perhaps they did not realise it, both were striving to keep command of themselves; both had reached a certain limit of endurance.

Desperately they fought pure instinct and overmastering impulse—and something that could be stronger than all will—than all things in the world.

The want of understanding kept the woman from speaking, and pride—ever the enemy of love —held the man silent. After all that had passed between them in that Turkish palace, they were about to part; to part with cold words.

"I'll come—if I can." He turned. "You understand, Daphnne?"

Again she struggled for speech; then spoke only a few cold, decisive words.

"I understand. I'll be ready—when you come."

"Till tonight, then. Hide those clothes now, and be careful of the women."

Abruptly, with the words, he went swiftly, with a jingle of spurs, across the rug-strewn floor and stepped out of the apartment.

* * *

Daphnne had never thought it possible that she would sleep that night, and yet sleep she did.

When she awoke it was he who awakened her, in a darkness that seemed the darkness of midnight.

He was bending over her, beside the bed, but a vague grey figure in the darkness.

"Oh, is it time?" She started up.

"Nearly," his level, utterly familiar voice answered her softly, swiftly. "Are you dressed?"

To him she was only a small, pale form upon the gorgeous cushions of the bed.

"Yes." She came quickly to her knees, clad in cotton trousers and a loose jacket of many folds.

"There is good time then. I thought perhaps you wouldn't dress till I came. But as you're ready, we'll go."

It was the first time they had been together in that inner room since that unforgetable night. Now—was it to be the last?

"Come!" he exclaimed, abruptly.

He took hold of her to help her from the bed and she held to him to get off the soft, yielding cushions. It was fatal—that touch.

They swayed suddenly together. He had her in his arms and his lips came down upon hers—close upon her mouth, which was raised swiftly to him.

Silence enveloped the Eastern palace, yet the very intensity of that silence seemed to reveal stealthy sounds, soft murmurs—a sense of unrest.

For passion-filled, throbbing moments they clung together in the darkness of the inner room—then reason strove to get command. He let her go, forced her from him, dragged his mouth from the sweetness of hers.

"Oh, come—!"

With one swift, sudden movement he lifted her from the bed. Passing through the curtains, they stepped into the bigger apartment.

"We must not fail now!" his fierce whisper came above her head. "You've just got to get away!"

Holding her hand, he led her through other luxurious apartments, across and down winding passages. Here and there a lamp flickered but mostly the soft, warm darkness enveloped them.

Turning a corner, they came upon a Turk sprawled motionless across a passage.

With a scarcely smothered cry the girl stopped, gripped the man. He released her clinging fingers with a reassuring touch.

"Hashish," he said briefly.

He led her on, down narrow stairs.

By a door which had glass panels giving eerie light, a small form seemed to leap out of the shadows; the form of a wizened little man almost hidden in a robe of blue.

The girl gasped again, but Ahmad Hadi strode to him.

"All is well? They are free—out there—?"

"They await, O Master," a thin, cracked voice answered from the blue robe.

"Ah." The man drew a swift breath.

He flung a glance over his shoulder, then looked back to the huddled little native, the only being in all the palace whom he had been able to trust with surety, having saved him when the Bey had ordered him to be flogged to death.

"Ramez, none suspect?"

"O My Lord, who should suspect? But away, O Master." The little form sprang to the door, dragged it open, and showed the dusk of clear night beyond.

Catching the cold, trembling hand of the girl, Ahmad Hadi drew her with him through the doorway and so out of the palace.

Swiftly, without pause, the man led her through the dusky, scent-filled garden. They came to a gate; heard faintly the jingle of horses' bridles.

The brightness of the sky gave light to the

earth and as she went through the gate Daphnne saw at once the three men who waited in the road with five horses.

The Englishmen: her father, Hadley, and Marsh! In the dusk of the night they looked three ghost-like figures before the no less ghostly-looking horses.

Colonel Wayne's cry could not be checked as he sprang towards his daughter.

"Father!" she gasped, and flung out her hands towards him.

Only for a moment was she clasped in his arms. The man who had brought her from the palace almost dragged her from her father.

"Be quick! You can't stop now—can't say a word!"

He lifted her, swung her easily up onto one of the horses.

"Listen! Was that—?"

In the night's stillness there came plainly slight sounds from the palace—the murmur of voices—

"My God!" burst out the man in grey. "They must have found out! Quick!"

The tone of his voice sent the three men into their saddles.

Daphnne, sitting astride her horse in her masculine Turkish dress, between her father and Hadley, looked to the man who had planned their escape.

She saw him hesitate by the gate. His horse, the only one riderless, a big black stallion, a superb animal, curveted to him and pushed a soft nose into his shoulder.

He turned then, caught the hanging reins,

and swung himself into the saddle. Only then did she draw up her own reins. The five horses sprang away from the gate with a thud of hoofs on sandy ground.

There was just sufficient light for the roadway to be discerned, and the five rode dangerously, urging their horses to a gallop.

The road joined another which ran from the front of the palace. Galloping upon this other road, they heard noises which rang even above the sounds of their own animals. The clattering of horses' hoofs which shattered the quietness of the night.

They swept into that other road, checking a little—and that party of horsemen, coming from the courtyard of the palace, appeared out of the darkness, almost on them.

Yells, coming from the throats of the Turks sent to recapture them, rent the air.

There was no time for any considered plan or mutual action. The Turks, yelling, were riding down upon them with fiercely swinging spurs and half-maddened horses.

Ahmad Hadi forced his big stallion across the road nearest to the Turks. He jerked his head, flung out his arm to the Englishmen.

"Ride for it!" he gasped.

Hadley and Daphnne were almost in the hedge on one side. Wayne and Marsh, the farthest from the Turks, hesitated for just the fraction of a minute—and then they went.

What it cost them to go only they, in that agonising moment, knew. Every instinct within them bade them remain, but reason urged them to go.

There was no hope of resisting the numbers of the Bey's men, and in the hands of the Turks they would all be helpless, but if they could escape, if only one of them could win free and get in communication with the British, then help could be got for the others in the Turk's power.

Jerking their horses round, they spurred them down the roadway, leaving the woman and the other men.

The foremost Turks, now just on the English party, swung rifles down from their shoulders and levelled them.

Ahmad Hadi, seeing the pale gleam of the weapons, swerved his horse across the road and brought the big black animal rearing into the air.

The Turks shouted and he shouted back to them. Only one rifle cracked, for they feared to hit him upon the rearing horse.

Kicking and rearing into the air, he kept the big furious stallion swerving across the roadway, checking the Turks who came upon them.

Daphnne, swaying in her saddle, cried out. In that moment she found her anxiety for the son of the Turk greater even than that for her father. His safety, it seemed, was more to her than that of her father.

As she saw him so recklessly playing with death she cried out gaspingly. She was agonisingly aware that he was willing even to give his own life to purchase their freedom—their safety.

His life was dearer—more precious—than anything else in the world. And he risked it so! Up and over went the big black horse, and as it fell the man sprang clear, rolling over on the ground to the grass at the side of the road.

The Turks were past him but the two Englishmen were far down the road. Rifles leapt again to shoulders, cracked, spat into the dusk.

But the darkness swallowed up the riders as if it had taken them from the earth.

Again the rifles cracked, then they were swung to shoulder and the foremost Turks spurred down the road in pursuit.

The girl swayed from her saddle and went without resistance into the hold of the Turks who surrounded her.

Only when she saw him, who had fallen from the big horse, rise assisted by three natives did life seem to stir again within her.

* * *

Ahmad Hadi did not give up all hope. Even when the palace loomed up above them he did not give way to despair. There was still, he thought, one chance for them; and everything depended upon that chance.

The revolver he always carried with him rested still beneath the sash under his coat. He had not drawn it out, had not fired a shot.

Just the thought of that last hope, that one more chance of safety for the two who remained in the Bey's power, kept his hand from the weapon.

He was the son of the Turk. In that their chance lay.

He had not openly checked the Turks. He had made it seem that his horse did the checking. His cries to them had been to the effect that he was striving to stop the English.

Hadley and the girl were led to the palace. He walked free—but the Turks surrounded him.

The two captives were pushed through the archway into the hall. Ahmad Hadi was immediately behind them.

The hall held a multitude of Turks. His glance flashed over them—and he gasped.

In the midst of that crowd of Turks, his face a distorted mask of fury, stood Sueleman Bey.

Beside the Bey, gesticulating, was a slim young Turk, the real Ahmad Hadi, the son of the Turk, the man whose place he, Julian Conquest, had taken.

The last hope, the last chance for them, was crushed. The thing he had never suspected, never thought of, had happened. For a moment he gasped—and then he acted.

Acted as swift as thought; with the swiftness born of desperation.

She was near him, slightly behind him. Hadley was before him, held by Turks.

With a suddenness and quickness that took the natives about him off their guard, he jerked the revolver from the sash under his coat, stepped back, flung his arm about the waist of the girl, and leapt with her to the wall.

Holding her to him; he set his back to the wall and levelled the weapon.

For one moment he thought of turning the weapon upon her and then upon himself. It would rescue her from the unthinkable fate—and for him it would be a merciful death.

When the Bey set hands upon them they would be dead. But all the eager youth in him cried out against this—stayed his hand.

133

He might have to use the weapon upon her
—and upon himself—but not yet, not yet.

The girl understood.

She had seen the infuriated Bey, had seen
the young Turk who stood beside him—slim, dark,
good-looking—strikingly like this man who was
near her.

She knew them both; he who was beside her
and the young Turk beside the Bey. Both had
been together in the Café Orient.

In a flash of revelation she understood. The
truth leapt upon her, paralysing her for a moment,
so that she was a stiff, motionless figure against
the man who held her.

There stood the real son of the Turk, and he
beside her was the white man.

Daphnne understood.

She saw, too, how great a thing it was he
had done; was conscious of the daring of it; realised what it meant to him—what had rested upon
his shoulders.

The barrier was down. What had been a
cruel check upon her love was gone. The awful
doubt that had crushed her heart with agony was
no more.

The stiffness went out of her small form; she
went close against him. Slowly her head went
back and she looked up at him.

The clamour of the Turks had ceased. The
tense silence, which had fallen on the man's swift
action, still held.

The man looked down into the girl's eyes and
read in them the message that only a man can
read in the eyes of a woman.

A message that drew him up from the depth

of bitterness and anguish and sent a thrill of fire through his blood, a surge of feeling to his heart.

"Daphnne!" he gasped.

And her answer came with a sobbing catch of breath.

"Julian—oh, Julian!"

Then, with greater violence, the clamour broke out again in the hall, and Conquest—for Conquest he was—dragged his look from the girl, up again to the Turks, and steadied the revolver he held.

Chapter Eight

Ahmad Sueleman Bey stood in the centre of the hall, choking with fury.

Beside him, his son told of how he had been tricked, waylaid, set upon in Trenedad, shut up in some hidden house there, by that other slim, dark man who stood now within the hall.

The Bey's rage left him incapable of speech.

All his heart and soul he had thrown into a great work of evil. And at long last the reward of his evil labours seemed his. He had but to stretch out his hand to grasp it—

Then, even as he stretched out, the success he strove to attain was dashed suddenly from his reach.

He had been so sure of that success that he had not even considered failure.

While he had planned and schemed with daring to overthrow the English, one of them had planned and schemed with a resourcefulness and daring that had outmatched his own!

While he believed them utterly in his power, one had penetrated to his province, had got within his very palace, had been given all his, the Bey's, confidence!

A red mist seemed to surge up before the

Turk's eyes when his thoughts dwelt on this.

And this white dog—who had outwitted him with cunning and daring greater than his own—was a boy—a slim, dark boy from whom he could, with ease, have crushed the life with his hands!

And the woman—the woman had been given to this man.

He, the Bey, had given her to him, thinking that he gave her to a fate that she, with her proud white birth and breeding, would think worse than death.

But he had given her to safety—had given her to one of her own race! But the end was not yet! The white dog had been revealed; was still within his power!

Fiercely, desperately, Sueleman Bey struggled for calmness; struggled to subdue the blind, mad rage that was clouding his mind.

That pause, short as it was, gave the boy who stood with his back to the wall his chance. He saw that the natives stood so that there was a clear path between him and the big Turk.

He drew his arm from about the girl, stepped a little forward, and took aim at Sueleman Bey.

"Stay where you are or I'll kill you where you stand!" he said, and in the big hall his words sounded with menacing curtness in the silence that fell as he moved.

"You others—make so much as a movement and I'll drop your master where he stands."

A hiss of fury came from Sueleman Bey. His arms jerked spasmodically but he did not dare to move with that steady-held revolver levelled at him.

"Release him!" Conquest flung out his left

hand towards the Turks who held Hadley.

The natives' hands relaxed; the Captain struggled fiercely from their hold.

"Go—you two! Quickly." Conquest spoke to the Englishman and the girl behind him.

"Get out of the palace—and you may be able to get horses. It's a chance, anyway. I'll hold them as long as I can. Go—quickly!"

"But—" Hadley strode forward and stopped, looking at the other man.

"Think of her!"

"I understand." Swiftly Hadley turned and caught the hand of the girl, who had taken a step forward.

Conquest kept the revolver levelled. He did not look at her, did not take his eyes for a moment from the Turk. Her glance clung to him.

Daphnne held back—and then suddenly yielded, let the Captain draw her with him between the Turks. The very fierce insistence of that other's beloved voice made her go without question.

To the very last he was utterly unselfish! His only thought was for saving her! He endeavoured to send her to safety while he himself remained to meet some awful death at the hands of the maddened Turk!

And he sent away, to assist her, the other man who could have stayed to fight with him. He would give his life for hers.

Seeing him as he faced the Turks—so stiff and motionless—noting all the ardent life, the grace and youth and beauty of him, Daphnne could have screamed aloud.

Not for one moment did she intend going, however.

Before, in that old life of hers, she might have accepted this man's sacrifice, but not now. Everything was changed now. A thousand times she preferred death with him to life at the price of leaving him.

Had she hurried with her companion she might have escaped with Hadley from the hall.

Sueleman Bey stood struggling with his rage. It was not the first time he had been in a position like this. Before, his nimble wits had got him safely out.

He dropped, suddenly, full length upon the Persian rugs.

Conquest's revolver roared immediately. But the shot went over him and brought down a Turk beyond him.

The tension snapped. The silence was shattered by a roar which seemed to come from the voices of fiends rather than human beings.

The men at the end of the hall leapt upon Hadley and the girl, while the others surged upon that other white man.

Springing back to the wall, Conquest fired until every chamber of his revolver was empty.

Turk after Turk he brought down before him. At such close quarters he could not miss—and without mercy he aimed to kill.

With their dead upon the floor before that one slim, young white man whom they thought must possess the power of the Evil One, the Turks checked a moment.

The Bey's voice urged them on, however, and,

with greater fury, with maniac yells, they returned to the attack.

Down the hall, Hadley was struggling in the midst of other natives. For a short while he had kept them from the girl, but their numbers prevailed and a blow from a knife-hilt brought him to the floor.

Two big harem attendants sprang forward and seized her.

Conquest fired his last shot and then, without waiting for the Turks to reach him, sprang forward, hurling himself into their midst.

Taken unawares, he was in them and through them before they realised they had touched him.

Springing upon a rug, he slid with it across the shining floor.

At the foot of the wide staircase, before he could rise from the rug on which he had come down, other Turks were upon him.

Sueleman Bey, now upon his feet, with a revolver gripped in one hand, shouted to his men with snarling lips.

As he left the wall, Julian had endeavoured to reach the stairs. Without looking he knew that Daphnne had not escaped. So now he would have to fight—fight as he had never fought before.

Daphnne herself had been dragged by the two eunuchs into the centre of the hall near the Bey and his son. For herself she had no fear; all her anxiety was for that man who fought at the foot of the stairs.

For a moment, wild confusion reigned.

Then Conquest fought out of their midst, struggled to reach the stairs.

On the instant Sueleman Bey swung up his revolver and took aim.

Quick as the Turk moved, the girl saw and moved quicker.

She had now no fear of the Bey. Something utterly fierce and primitive in her flung her forward like a flash of pale light upon the Turk's arm.

His aim was marred; the shot, meant for the white man, brought down one of his own natives.

With a hiss of fury the Bey turned upon her and strove to fling her from him. But she clung still, holding down his arm.

He swung up his free hand and hit her on the soft, white brow where the gold curls clustered. She reeled from him and the eunuchs dragged her back into their charge.

Conquest, with three natives holding to him, had reached the stairs. With two swift-swung blows he felled first one and then the other, and, kicking out savagely, caught the third with a riding-boot, sending the native back upon those behind, which brought them to the ground.

Tearing from him the grey coat, he flung it away and stood a slim, supple figure in light shirt and breeches.

He was laughing a little, fiercely, mockingly, and his golden eyes gleamed with the joy of the fight.

Indeed, the young Lieutenant almost took pleasure in that fierce conflict. All the youth and virile life in him leapt to meet that wild moment.

And, with the knowledge in his heart which the girl's unspoken message had given him, he felt able to combat even that horde of Turks.

He fought for something now which was as precious as life. Having gained the stairs, he had a slight advantage. He turned and, swift-footed, fled up the staircase.

Reaching the stairhead, he turned. The foremost Turks were almost upon him. Springing to the balcony at one side, he seized a gorgeous shawl and flung it down upon them.

The silken folds descended, enveloping them, blinding them. They stumbled on the stairs, bringing others down with them.

Sueleman Bey had moved up to the girl now in the hold of the eunuchs. His dark face, now distorted with malicious rage, came down to the pale, fair loveliness of hers.

"Did you think I kill him?" he snarled. "Did you think I take aim to kill? No. I take aim only to maim—to bring him down! Did you think I give him that swift, sudden death? No—no! He dies slowly—slowly!"

Sueleman Bey leapt back as a large, priceless vase, flung from the balcony, crashed to a hundred pieces on the tessellated floor almost at his feet.

Even with the Turks in pursuit of him the lover had seen in the hall her, his beloved, shrinking from the leering Bey.

Conquest had given the natives a chance to overtake him, though, and they were almost upon him now on the balcony. Turning for flight, he saw, coming from the right wing of the balcony, more Turks.

He was caught between the two parties. His capture seemed a thing beyond question. For a moment he hesitated, then, springing to the balustrade, he swung himself over and jumped.

Daphnne gasped as she saw him leap from the height of the balcony to the floor of the hall.

But Conquest had judged his leap for a wide couch which was beneath the balcony.

He came full length upon the cushions and rolled over amidst their splendour onto the floor. Only slightly shaken, he gained his feet and stood, hesitating, looking towards the Bey, the Bey's son, and the girl.

The Turk's big body stiffened; he stood waiting, with a snarling curl to his full lips.

The natives decided Conquest's next move for him. With yells the remaining men in the hall hurled themselves towards him.

He sprang across the couch, dodged them a moment round the pillars of the balcony, then turned for a curtained entrance and was gone from sight.

The natives surged into the entrance on his heels. The Bey, still with that awful look of hate and glee upon his face, stood between his son and the imprisoned girl.

A little farther down the hall, half-a-dozen remaining Turks stood about the motionless form of the other Englishman.

The Bey flung orders to these latter. Lifting Hadley's bound figure, they carried him from the hall.

Fury surged up in Daphnne, a fury she could not control. She had never thought it possible that she, so civilised and conventional, could know so wild a passion.

Like a small, fair creature possessed, she struggled, writhing light-clad limbs, tossing short gold hair. Twisting, she set small teeth in the fat

143

arm of the eunuch who sought to grip her round the waist.

With a howl he let go of her completely, and, tearing herself from the other's grasp, she sprang away and fled for the nearest entrance.

Passing through the curtains, she fled down a long chamber.

But her shoulder caught a screen and the blow, combined with the pain in her head from that other blow from the Turk's fist, dazed her a moment.

Before she recovered, the Turks caught her.

A big eunuch pushed forward, gripped her, lifted her, swung her across his shoulder, and carried her back to the hall.

Evil glee mastered rage in the Bey's look as he regarded the limp, now almost-bare body of the girl lying across the muscular shoulder of the big native.

He flung an order to the eunuch. The fellow turned, carried her up the hall, up the stairs, and to her old apartment.

* * *

Daphnne was dropped upon her feet in the big room of her old apartment. The eunuch hurried out.

The girl swayed a little as she gained her balance, turned, and, with wild passion, flung herself against the panel door.

With small, white hands she tore at the intricate pattern of the immovable, panelled, Eastern door until her soft fingers were bruised and cut.

Exhausted, she sank to the floor, a small, panting, huddled figure.

Crouched there, she thought of him. Everything was so plain before her now. She could not get from her mind the thought of what he had done.

The boldness and the daring of his action held her mute. He had taken the place of the son of the Turk—to get into the province and palace of Sueleman Bey.

He, Julian Conquest, had dared the peril of the scheme to get to them and try to effect their rescue.

And he was the man to whom she had never shown the least kindness. His warning she had laughed at; they had parted with hostility. Yet he risked all—to save her!

She thought of their meeting in that Turkish palace. After he had dared so much, risked so much, she had been utterly without gratitude.

She had turned on him with bitter fury, had lashed him with her tongue—and he had been risking all, alone, to save them!

Daphnne crouched on the floor and sobbed a little with a choking breath.

"Oh, what a beast I was!" she gasped. "How could I have been so horrid—?"

He had been so unselfish and kind and chivalrous.

And she—she had been utterly selfish. She had taken all from him—and had given nothing.

It seemed to her, as she crouched by that shut door, that all her past life had been selfishness. She had never known the joy of giving. But now—now she longed only to give.

Now—Daphnne realised that now Love could make her suffer for all her past selfishness.

Now he was the whole world for her; nothing else mattered.

Love . . . love that was an intense, poignant pain throbbed in her heart with every difficult, sobbing breath she drew. And perhaps now he would never know of her remorse; never know of the love for him which now filled her whole being.

She had let the time go; she had not understood when they held the precious moments. She had been blind when he had tried so hard to make her understand.

Now this love might never be.

But she could not think of this. Such love—that had been given to them—could not die—unfulfilled.

"Julian!" she gasped, her torn fingers pressed to the panel. "Oh, Julian!"

Dear brave heart that had risked so much for them!

Would he now have to pay the penalty?

"Oh, God, save him—don't let him die!"

The wild passion which shook her slender body utterly exhausted her. She sank down to the floor.

A slight click sounded and the panel came slowly open, pushing against her small, huddled figure.

She had just strength enough to get upon her feet and stand, her hands pressed to her breast.

Sueleman Bey stood in the entrance. He made no attempt to enter the room but remained in the doorway, looking at her with fierce, black glittering eyes.

"O woman of the arrogant white race," he said, "know that your schemes with the other white dog will come to naught. He is caught. He is, even now, writhing in the bonds of my power!"

Daphnne gave one short choking gasp.

Turning, Sueleman Bey went as abruptly as he had appeared. The panel door shut again securely.

Daphnne swayed upon her feet. She had just strength enough to reach the couch in the centre of the room and then she collapsed upon it.

Darkness descended upon her.

*   *   *

It seemed to Daphnne Wayne that she struggled for endless time in that enveloping darkness.

Her whole body felt racked with poignant pain; awful anguish possessed her soul.

Then—warm lips were pressed upon hers; strong arms slipped about her pain-filled body, lifting her up.

Strong, ardent life seemed to surge through her chilled form from those lips upon her own. When that kiss ended she gasped a little and opened her eyes.

Opened wide eyes to see him, for whom she suffered, bending over her. To see the dearly loved, dark, audacious face which she thought perhaps she would never again see in life.

Even then she could not believe, could not realise the truth, though she saw him kneeling beside her couch with his arms about her.

He bent and kissed her again and the warmth and strength of his lips upon hers told her of quick, throbbing life!

She started up; her hands slipped across his dark, clear-cut face, his youthful head with the dark hair all disordered, the dear, slim, lithe form of him; and, feeling all the power of supple muscles, the warm, quick life of his strong body, she gasped with thrilling gladness.

He was safe! He was alive and here beside her!

With a choking cry her arms went about him; she clung to him with all the strength left in her soft, weary little form.

"Julian!" she gasped.

"Daphnne!" he said with all the joy of life in his tone. "Oh, child of my heart."

Shivering, sobbing, she clung to him, almost choking him with the tightness of her arms about his neck, and the man wondered a little at her wild agitation.

The ecstasy of that moment commanded all thought and feeling. Her warm, beautiful body was pressed to his, her soft arms were folded about his neck, her cheek was against his.

The passion with which she clung to him filled him with an exquisite, scarce-endurable delight.

"Oh, Julian," she gasped after a while, "they said—they said—"

"Yes?" he murmured.

"They said they had captured you. The Turk . . . the beast! . . . he said he had got you. That you were captured, and . . . oh, Julian, I nearly died!"

"Daphnne!" he cried. "Child—did it matter so much?"

"Oh, Julian, I was in hell . . . and you came and lifted me out of it."

He crushed her against his heart. He would

have spoken but no words could be found for that moment.

"If you hadn't come . . . I think I should have died!" she said.

He bent and pressed his cheek to her short gold curls. He had hardly dared to believe that this exquisite moment would ever be his.

He had found the soul of this sweet, lovely child; had awakened her to the meaning of love. He was conscious of a thrill through his whole being; a wild joy and exulting gladness in his heart.

"Dear," he said, "you care—you care—?"

Her arms came about him, warm and close, clinging with a passion that thrilled him. She had had so much to say, to tell him, but she could only gasp a few words, yet they were sufficient.

"Oh, Julian, I love you! . . . I love you!"

He let her back on the couch and his lips on hers thrilled her.

Time stood still to the command of Love.

They had no thought for the peril that completely surrounded them; each was wrapt in the presence of the other, both in the glory of their love.

Yet every blissful moment that they lost was dear to them; their danger increased with every swiftly passing minute.

But the man who had been conscious of their peril for so many weary days gave no thought to it now.

He was held in the thrall of triumphant love. She was his!

She belonged to him now—this fair, lovely

child who yet possessed all the glory of womanhood.

"Darling," he whispered. "You love—?"

"Oh, Julian . . . so much now! I love you . . ."

He held her to him and kissed her again. The passion of his lips, the desire she felt in the clinging pressure of his mouth on hers, aroused no fear in her now but only a strange, wild joy.

An answering passion surged in her own slight form.

"I think I've loved you for so long," she said. "I fought against that love but . . . oh, it was so sweet to know, in the hall, that I'd no need to fight anymore. . . ."

He took her hands, kissed each finger, pressed his lips to the soft palms. She let her cheek rest against his dark hair.

"Child," he murmured. "So even the Turk knew, even he understood; he knew he could hurt you by saying I was captured. Oh, my dearest!" He pressed warm kisses on her pale cheeks, her bare throat, her soft, white shoulders that the straps of the small, pearl-covered jacket did not cover.

His passion, which once had been wild, was now softened with the gentleness of love, was tender with the knowledge of conquest.

"Dearest," he repeated, looking up with eyes that had the gleam of gold, "did you think I would let myself be captured, with the knowledge of your love in my heart?"

She raised herself a little in his arms and looked at him.

"Dear," she murmured, "what does it mean?

Oh, Julian, where are they? How have you got away—?"

He drew himself from her, sat back on his heels, and laughed a little, slim hands on his hips, the old audacious, half-arrogant look in his golden eyes.

"Daphnne, I gave them the devil of a chase over the palace roof. The Bey'll be having a fit now. I wanted to get to you," his voice deepened a little, "so I eluded them on the roof and—found you."

His arms came about her again but her hands had slipped up to his shoulders, feeling the dear, lithe, slender form of him for any hurt.

He showed, indeed, evidence of the wild fight he had come through. His white shirt was torn in ribbons down from one shoulder, showing a bare, tanned throat and the strong, supple body that she loved.

On the other side it clung to the shoulder with a dark stain of crimson. A slight cut marred one bronzed cheek.

"Oh, you're hurt!" she gasped.

"It's nothing, Daphnne," he said. "Dearest, do you think I'd mind such hurts if I might have the sweet caress of your hands upon me?"

Her hands faltered a little then.

"Julian," she said, and there was again the quiver of passion in her voice. "Julian, you've done all this, you've done so much for me—oh, am I worth it?"

"You know what you are worth!" he said, holding her with a quick passion. "Darling, you're so lovely—you know what you have to give—"

"But, Julian, I was so horrid to you. I was a little beast—"

"No, dear—"

"Yes, I was. Julian," her arms came again about his neck, her soft cheek pressed to his, "Julian, can you forgive me?"

"Forgive you! Child, how can you talk of forgiveness between us—when we love?"

"But I was such a little beast to you, Julian. I didn't know all the dear goodness of your heart. I didn't know your wonderful unselfishness. I never gave you one kind word—"

He tilted back her gold head to look into her eyes.

"Was that because you knew you'd have to give yourself to me one day?"

"I . . . I believe it was," she whispered back with a faint, unsteady laugh. "I think I knew, in my heart, when we first met, that I'd seen the man to whom I should belong. I think I knew I couldn't escape you . . . if you claimed me. And because I was so selfish and independent, I . . . I think I hated you."

He laughed, the soft, happy laughter of conquest.

"I, too, knew you were the woman—I wanted. But because I thought you a vain, pampered child, I also was angry. But, dear, it was meant from the first that we should love. And we love now, we hold the future—"

Jarring, confused sounds in the palace had increased; a disturbing murmur of subdued clamour came into the chamber—as if to emphasise the uncertainty of that future of which he spoke.

Yet still they did not heed, lost in a world of

their own—a world made up of Love. He tilted back her head and laughed a little with bright golden eyes looking into her grey ones.

"Did you hate being kissed by the Turk's son? Did you hate—my kisses—?"

"They hurt me a little, but—oh, I didn't hate them as I ought to have done! And they ... they altered life for me."

"I couldn't let you go from me, Daphnne. When you deliberately went off with the Turk, I tried to forget you. As if I could! I tried to convince myself that I did this daring thing to get into the Turk's palace for your father—but it was for you. I suffered hell thinking of you in the hands of that fiend—at his mercy. I didn't care what I did—what I risked—to get to you—my woman!"

"You saved me," she whispered, small white hands caressing his dark hair. "If you hadn't come, oh, my dear, you know what I'd have suffered, what would have been my fate!"

"Dear," he said with quick fierceness, and his arms hurt her a little with their strength, "don't speak of it! I—I would have killed you—to save you from the Turk—but, thank God, I succeeded another way—"

"I would have welcomed death ... at your hand...."

"Darling—I would not give you death—but life!"

"I know how much I owe you," she went on. "Even that night ... oh, my dear, you'll never know how I love you for that! You were so good to me! Before then I was still blind, still proud, but that night I knew ... I was but a woman. And you were so dear and generous. You saved me . . . spared me. . . ."

"Child," he drew a little away from her; his golden eyes darkened and faint lines showed by his even mouth, "you don't understand. I spared you—yes. But it cost me a struggle; a struggle in which I nearly lost—the wrong way. There wasn't much goodness in my heart—that night. I wanted you. I had to fight myself—and I nearly lost."

"I know . . ."

"You knew?"

"Dear," she said, "do you think a woman doesn't know when a man fights for her like that?"

"So you knew?" he whispered. "I wanted you—?"

"I knew what it cost you to give me up," she said, as low. "Oh, I know how you suffered. And you won. Dear, I love you so much for that. Before that night I was still angry with you, but after . . . after, I could only love you. You could have done what you liked with me, Julian. . . ."

"Daphnne!" he said hoarsely, and his eyes were still dark. "But I so nearly played a vile part that night. There was a wildness in me that I'm ashamed of now. But, dear, there was something that gave me the strength to fight myself—you, coming to me in the hall. You had given yourself to me; how could I be a beast and harm you?"

He gathered her closer in his arms.

"Dear, I've thought so much, I've wondered—why did you do that? Why did you come to me? You thought I was the Turk's son. But you came to me—fled to my arms. Why, Daphnne?"

She smiled a little, dark grey eyes half-closed.

"It was something in me I couldn't control. My reason saw peril everywhere, but my heart ... my heart, Julian, must have known where there was safety for me."

"Dearest!" His voice was low, with a subdued fierceness. "I'd have shot him that night if he'd used force to take you—"

"Julian!" She spoke his name with a low, thrilling tone that made the man catch his breath. "Ah, my dear, I need not have feared; you were guarding me so well."

"But, dear," he stopped her, "I so nearly gave in. How can you speak like that, knowing how I—I nearly made you mine that night! I wanted you. I could have been vile enough to have gloried in my strength—and your weakness. I was—was little better than the Turk, dear. I could have stayed with you—could have made you mine! If the dawn hadn't come—"

"I know, dear," she whispered, slim hands against his throat. "But the dawn came—"

He held her close in his arms.

"Yes, child, the dawn came—and, oh, my dear, I'm glad. Because I waited, I have now so great a reward. Instead of hating me—you love me!"

He pressed his lips upon hers, and her lovely, quivering mouth beneath his responded with answering passion.

Her small hands slipped across his shoulders; her slight, beautiful body pressed to his slim, lithe form. He felt the beat of her heart under his, her pulses throbbing with all the joy of youthful life. ...

And the murmur of confused sounds in the

palace increased still more. The precious moments slipped by unheeded. Peril closed swiftly in about them.

"Darling—you understand at last?" he whispered. "Love—"

"Julian," she murmured back, "I understand now. I know what love can be ... and I long ... as much as you. ..."

His slender fingers slipped through her short gold hair.

"You have been so dear and unselfish, but now it will be my glory to give—"

He pressed his lips to hers again. All the youthful blood in him leapt at her words with a fire that would not be subdued.

The noise which had been continuous and discordant increased to loudness. It came into the room on the air from the terrace—came from the roof above.

It disturbed the man and he released the woman and moved back a little uneasily.

"Oh, Julian, you've altered all the world for me ... I can't lose you now! If you're hurt ... if you're caught ..."

Yet more the noise above increased, and now Conquest sprang lightly to his feet; lifted the girl from the couch to her feet with a quick movement which sent a stab of hot pain through his wounded shoulder.

"Daphnne, don't talk of death—but life—life for us now!"

"Yes, but—"

"Child, we hold the world now!"

His fingers tightened round her slim hand. With golden eyes gleaming he threw back his head with an eloquent gesture, and, despite her fear, her young, ardent spirit leapt to meet his.

"Daphnne, we must fight for our love—fight as we fought before. Can you—?"

Her small hand tightened about his. Her grey eyes sparkled, meeting his golden ones. In her stiffening figure there was all the assurance and determination of the modern West.

"Yes, Julian."

The noise above became clamour; a hideous clamour that rang down to the terrace. Yelling, native voices sounded and dark, jumbled shadows fell across the white terrace.

Conquest leapt over the couch and flung himself against the panel of the door.

"Oh, it's useless!" Daphnne gasped a little, hands pressed to her throat. "I've tried; you can't open it—"

But his strong slender fingers went swiftly over the pattern, up the side of the panel. There came that faint click and it swung slowly open.

She was at his side immediately. He caught her hand, dragged her into the anteroom, and pulled shut the panel just as a crowd of Turks surged across the chamber from the terrace.

It was a near thing. The lovers both knew that.

The yelling Turks surged through the panel door and went down the passage after them. The little start they had obtained in getting out of the girl's chamber was so slight as to be hardly worth considering.

As they closed doors behind them the Turks were always just at the other side. The least check for them meant capture.

Striving desperately to throw off that yelling

crowd which was almost on them, Conquest leapt between the entrance curtains and out to the hall, with the girl behind him.

On either side of the entrance, dark forms rose swiftly and flung themselves upon him before he could make the least movement of defence. He went down beneath them.

Daphnne smothered a scream. The palace hall showed still the disorder caused by the previous fight.

By the big couch in the centre stood Sueleman Bey, mad hate and fury gleaming still in his eyes.

On the couch sat his slim, good-looking son, his eyes narrowed and bright. The Bey's impassive chief men stood at some little distance from the couch.

In one of the chambers adjoining the hall, Captain Hadley lay still a helpless captive. Conquest fought madly, forcing them to give up all thought of overpowering him without a struggle.

A savage rage was in his heart, and a fear he had never felt before. He had not expected capture so soon. Yet, for all his youth and strength and arrogance, that previous fight had taxed his powers of endurance—and he was wounded.

Stabs of awful pain went through his shoulder as their ruthless hands grasped it, and a faintness came upon him.

Sueleman Bey came across the floor to the outskirts of that *mêlée*. Hate and fury and malicious joy on his face made it look the dark countenance of a fiend.

A sick terror was in Conquest's heart when he realised what his capture would mean. The Turk's triumph would put the Englishmen in that country in great peril, and the woman he loved would be left to the mercy of the Turks.

That second thought aroused him to a madness that not even the Turks could conquer. He must not give in!—must not lose!

Daphnne herself gave little thought to their position; all her attention was upon the man she loved; all her fear was for what he would suffer upon capture.

When two eunuchs seized her and tried to drag her into the centre of the hall, she too resisted with wild passion. Sueleman Bey, looking from the struggling girl to the man who fought his Turks so savagely, smiled an evil smile.

The Turks overpowered him at last. They held him helpless as he lay upon the floor, exhausted in their midst. Yells and cries of triumph rang down the hall and then died to silence as Sueleman Bey took command.

Looking down upon his helpless captive, the Turk laughed— and his laughter brought a choaking cry from the white girl's lips. The Bey flung orders to his men and they dragged the slim, wounded form of the white man to his feet.

Conquest looked to the girl. Daphnne looked to him. Their glances met. Both realised then that all their chances of escape were lost; that they were helpless in the power of the Bey.

Instinct moved them both; they acted simultaneously. He tore himself from the hands of the Turks; she slipped from the hold of the eunuchs. They came together.

Before the Turks had even realised their intention, the white man and girl were clasped in each other's arms and their lips had met.

All the joy and anguish of the world seemed brought into that moment. The gladness of life and the bitterness of death was in that kiss.

All hope was lost. There was no further chance of rescue for them. Their love could never be. The wonderful love that had come into their lives could never now be gloriously fulfilled.

An exquisite rapture and a bitterness beyond belief was in that last embrace; an anguish scarcely endurable in that farewell kiss.

Heart to heart, lip to lip, they clung together.

With sudden hideous cried the Turks moved and flung themselves upon those two. But the lovers could not be parted. The man held the woman to him with almost superhuman strength, and her arms clung fiercely about his slim body.

The Turks renewed their efforts but only after a long moment did they succeed in parting those two who clung so fiercely to each other.

Struggling wildly, Conquest was drawn back.

"Forgive me—Daphnne," he gasped, "I would have saved you—"

"Oh, my dear . . . you did so much. . . ."

"To the pillar with him!" the Bey snarled in English. "Bind him firm to the post!"

The white man's slim form was dragged to one of the balcony pillars at the left side of the hall and the natives set about binding him to the pillar.

Above the subdued clamour the gasping voice of the girl came suddenly to the Turk.

"Sueleman Bey, is there nothing that will make you let him go? Is there no price . . . that I can pay . . . that'll make you let him . . . go free . . . ?"

The Bey turned and his black eyes fell upon the white, shivering woman in the hold of the eunuchs. She closed her eyes, not meeting his look, striving not to shrink.

"Aha," said the Turk, and his tone was full of significance.

"Daphnne!" Conquest cried out, and his voice rang down the hall.

She shivered; even her fair face was drawn with pain. The agony in the beloved voice was like a knife thrust into her heart.

"Daphnne, what are you saying—to him—" He could barely get out the words.

She drew herself up a little, looked for just one moment to him with her dark, heavy eyes.

"Dear, won't you let me . . . do this little . . . what I can . . . for you . . . ?"

"No, no, no!" Conquest cried out wildly.

Sueleman Bey strode up to the girl; regarded her with cruel, gloating eyes.

"So," he said, "you have a price—as all others—"

Slowly her eyes closed.

"Every woman has her price," said the Turk. "It is proved."

Her eyes came open and she faced him suddenly.

"Yes," she panted, "you're right. Every woman has a price. One price. The price that will pay for him she loves!"

"Daphnne!" Conquest's voice came hoarsely but in fierce command. "Be quiet!"

Sueleman Bey snarled.

"The man shall not go from me. He shall suffer for what he dared against me! And you—" he turned on the girl, "your fate will be whatever I decree and your will in the matter is as nothing!"

The Turks had bound Conquest to the pillar; bound him from shoulder to waist with cords that were cruel with their tightness.

With the burning pain of his shoulder, the exhaustion of his body, the torment of his mind, the added agony of those bonds made existence barely endurable.

With her last failing strength Daphnne struggled—struggled frantically to reach him—to get to him she loved.

The Turks drew back. The man's slender figure showed clearly bound to the post; a supple, well-formed body held fast to the straight pillar.

A white sacrifice to a dark fiend!

Sueleman Bey came slowly forward and with gloating eyes looked upon his captive.

He bent and brought his dark, convulsed face close to the drawn, rigid countenance of the other man. He spoke of the fate for that other—of the torture he would suffer—of the mutilation of that slim, shapely body—

Daphnne screamed. Her scream of horror and anguish rang down the length of the big palace hall. The Bey straightened and turned. A smile parted yet more his curling lips. That scream rang pleasantly in his ears.

Only on that scream did Conquest's hard, set face betray any expression, and then his golden eyes blazed.

"My God—you fiend!" he gasped. "Take the woman away!"

But the Bey was in no hurry to end the mental torture of his captives. It was pleasant to see the suffering of the lovely white woman and the slender white man, both of whom had defied and thwarted him.

The growling murmur of the Turks was faint in the hall. From without the palace the murmur of the village came with greater force; an almost disquieting murmur.

With a little shuddering cry the white girl sank unconscious in the arms of the eunuchs. Without moving, the Bey flung them an order. The eunuchs lifted her small, limp body and carried her from the hall.

Chapter Nine

Julian Conquest let his pain-tortured body droop in the cords that bound him.

Death—an awful death—faced him. And he did not want to die—yet.

Life had not given him all that he wanted. He had never known the love of a woman. Had never taken the pleasures which his warm, youthful life craved for and which his position and wanderings in the East had brought before him.

He had waited for a woman who could arouse pure passion within him. And he had found her. Had found her—too late! With his career so promising, with life so sweet before him—he had to die.

To die without knowing the joys of love that his young ardent body craved for! It was bitter.

It would have been less bitter had he saved her. From the first he had been willing to die to save her. But he had not accomplished even that—her safety. The thought was unendurable—the most agonising of all!

Death—

For him a hideous end.

For her—

Sueleman Bey's dark, now almost-repulsive

face was bent towards him. The Turk was speaking—torturing him with every hideous detail of that awful end that was to be his.

Conquest set his teeth and strove to keep his face expressionless. The Turks waited, ready to carry out their master's orders.

The murmur of the village could be heard plainly in the hall. A man hurriedly entered the palace from the wide courtyard.

Fiercely he pushed his way through the crowd of Turks. Three or four tried to stop him as he made for the Bey, but he came up to the big Turk and broke into a flood of agitated speech in the native tongue.

The Bey made a fierce gesture towards him to silence him. The native, however, continued to exclaim, waving his arms wildly. The Turk turned.

"Dog!" he shouted. "Wilt though speak to me when I bid thee be silent?" And he crashed a fist into the man's face, knocking him to the floor.

The native rolled over once and then lay still.

Sueleman Bey turned again to the torturing of his captive.

"And she—the fair woman you thought to cherish"—he spoke on, taking fiendish pleasure in what he said—"I gave her to you with certain orders! All that I said shall now be done to her!"

Tortured beyond endurance, Conquest retaliated. He was not bound below the waist and he kicked out savagely, catching the Turk with his riding-boot.

With an inarticulate cry the Bey went back. Recovering his balance, he started forward and swung up his fist to strike the pale, wild face of the man bound to the pillar.

Mastering himself, however, before the blow fell he turned to his Turks who had sprung forward with ready knives, waved them back, and gave them swift orders.

Julian knew he had hastened his end, but all he cared was that the awful torture of words should cease.

"Thou shalt suffer now—here in this hall," snarled the infuriated Bey. "Thou shalt die now slowly—slowly—"

One native, naked to the waist, kept hold of three thin knives; knives with long, tapering blades that, in a skilled hand, would not kill but could be used horribly.

The long, thin blades gleamed evilly in the light. Slowly one blade advanced—slowly came up to the bared, shapely breast of the white man— touched, cut the smooth, light skin—

Sueleman Bey stood, preparing to gloat—

His son laid a quick, dark hand upon his arm—

The murmur in the village had increased. A jarring noise arose suddenly in the courtyard without to join it. There came the disjointed crack of revolvers.

Clamour increased without. Voices were heard—jabbering natives voices—other voices; sharp, clear—English voices! Sueleman Bey had swung round, gasping a little.

Through the entrance into the hall came half-a-dozen figures—light-clad figures that there was no mistaking!

A din of awful sound—wild confusion—broke out immediately within the hall. The Turks

166

swarmed about the hall, looking towards the Englishmen who advanced with revolvers drawn.

Many of the natives looked to their master but Sueleman Bey was at that moment incapable of giving an order. He had staggered back towards the stairs, and his eyes—the eyes of a madman—stared at the figures of the hated white men.

Left to themselves, the Turks had to act on their own. But, without a leader, the confusion increased. A few flourished knives, sprang towards the Englishmen. Revolvers cracked again.

This, added to the suddenness of their appearance, completely dismayed the natives. Other white men could be seen in the entrance. The Turks thought all was lost.

Wild confusion broke out. There was a mad rush from the hall. And Sueleman Bey clung to the balustrade at the foot of the stairs and madness gleamed in his dilated eyes.

There can be no describing the wild tumult in the mind of the Turk. Only when the Englishmen entered the hall did he know that his plans were ruined.

And upon the floor, an inert figure still, lay the man who had sped to Sueleman Bey with the warning of the white men's presence in the village.

The mad tumult in the Bey's mind marred his reason. Out of the awful jumble of thoughts only two things stood clear: his hate of the English, and his desire to be avenged before the end.

The Turk thought of the white woman—the one sure way of vengeance upon the Englishmen —which they would never be able to forget!

While the natives surged from the hall in wild

flight from the English, he backed slowly up the stairs. Turning to the left, he walked softly round the balcony and slipped from sight between green curtains.

Julian Conquest had seen the Englishmen, and then had sunk unconscious in his cruel bonds against the pillar.

The Turk's son stood where he had turned to look down the hall. Erect and with little expression on his dark, handsome face, he watched the white men.

Amid the awful disorder in the big Eastern hall the Englishmen took command.

* * *

Daphnne Wayne sat on the floor beside the couch in the centre of the big apartment.

She looked to the sunlight. It was bright—glaring. The sky was blue—a hard, vivid blue. Nothing was beautiful. There was no more beauty in the world. Everything she looked at seemed to hurt. All was hard, brilliant, merciless!

There was no more beauty.

He was dead!

Her lover—the dear, brave boy of her heart—he was dead. His youth and beauty, his ardent life, all destroyed by a ruthless hand. His slim, strong, vital body now stiff and cold.

They had killed him! He had gone and left her to face life alone.

Life? Her heart was dead within her. How could she live when her heart was dead? A faint click sounded in the quietness of the chamber. The panel door came open and in came the Turk.

Life came suddenly back to her. Gripping the

couch, she dragged herself up. Her dilated glance was fixed upon the Turk. Madness showed in his gleaming eyes.

She steadied herself against the couch. Hate and horror were mingled in her heart.

In his eyes she read what her fate was to be. He had killed her lover—and now he came to take her! With hands red with the blood of her beloved he came to her!

Horor and hate deepened in her. Yet, knowing what her fate was to be, she was determined in some way to avoid it.

She belonged to the dear lover, even though he was dead, and she would go to him as he had left her in life. Before the Turk got her she would die.

As the Turk approached her she turned to move, but the Bey perhaps guessed her intention, for with a sudden, fierce spring he reached her and caught her.

Gripping her by her slender waist, he swung her across his shoulder and carried her from the room.

Through many apartments the Turk carried the white girl. Then, coming to a small spiral stairway, he began to ascend with her—up, up, a way that seemed never-ending.

The stairway ended at last, however, and he entered a small, round room. Setting the girl on her feet, he turned and closed the door.

Daphnne flung a swift glance round that small apartment. It was completely round and low-ceilinged. It had three windows which opened on to small balconies.

Only one of the three windows was open.

Looking to it, she saw pale blue sky and had an impression of the palace and gardens lying far, far below.

It seemed to her that she was utterly isolated with the maddened Turk.

What the girl did not know was that he had brought her to the small chamber that was at the very top of the big dome over the palace.

Cold with horror, she saw him lock and bolt the door. Then he turned and lurched towards her. With a choking cry she avoided him and sprang round the table.

On that awful journey on the Turk's shoulder she had not struggled but had reserved her strength for the fight that had to come.

That open window and the high balcony offered her the one way of escape she desired. But she had to get the chance to reach that balcony.

He pursued her round the table. The girl saw her chance and fled for the window and the balcony. But he was too quick for her. She had only got one knee upon the parapet when he reached her, dragged her back into the room.

The terror and horror gave her a wild strength. She struggled frantically in his arms, using her only weapons, teeth and sharp fingers.

As he loosened his hold she got from him and sprang for the balcony. But again he caught her. He gripped her shoulder, breaking one of the thin straps of her jacket, and dragged her into his arms.

She was helpless then. The strength she had found to fight was gone. She was exhausted, panting for breath.

He sank upon one of the seats with her, forced

her back in his arms. One of his hands was upon her throat and seemed to be choking the life from her—

Suddenly the brightness by the open window was darkened. A form came up from the blue void, over the balustrade to the balcony, and leapt from the balcony upon the big body of the Turk.

The girl slipped to the floor. For a while, she lay without attempting to move, panting, sobbing a little.

Slowly she became aware of those two who fought within the room. Looking at those two, she saw who it was who fought the Turk—a young, slim, half-clad man.

There was no wonder in her. It did not seem surprising that it should be he who had saved her who had come to her when she had been in such desperate need of help.

She did not know that the man, wounded though he was, had climbed from the terraced roof of the left wing right up the outside of the great green dome.

Holding herself upright to stand by the seat, she watched that fierce, awful fight, yet the savageness of it gave her no fear or repulsion at all.

Julian Conquest was a slender, almost small figure compared to the big, heavy form of the Turk, but indulgence, soft living, had spoilt the muscles of the Bey, while those of the younger man were flexible and strong as steel.

In the hearts of both was the knowledge that they must fight to the death. Over and over across the floor they rolled, grappling savagely, striving for mastery.

171

Coming up against the side of the wall, they struggled there for a moment and the big Turk got on top. A knife gleamed in his hand.

Crouching by the seat, the girl watched for a moment; then she flung herself upon the Turk, seized his arm with small, fierce hands. The knife, which would have found the breast, caught only the hip of the white man.

Struggling away from her as she stumbled back against the wall, they got free of each other.

Fighting savagely, they gained the little balcony and then again parted. The Turk still held the knife. He leapt forward and struck.

Conquest, avoiding the blow, went to his knees. The Bey, carried forward by the force of his thrust, lurched against the wooden parapet. There was the sound of a crack, a half-choked cry—

Turk and parapet vanished suddenly over the edge of the balcony. Silence settled upon the little chamber.

Conquest remained upon his knees, staring with expressionless, pain-darkened eyes into the blue void.

Sueleman Bey had gone to answer to a greater judge than any upon earth. Never would the Turk suffer in life for his evil deeds.

Fate, the schemer, the ruler of life and death, is inevitable. The Turk was gone. There was nothing more to be feared from him.

Yet there was still something more to be done. So thought the man. He was exhausted, almost deprived of the power to keep himself upright.

Yet he must not give in—dare not let consciousness slip from him yet!

There was still a duty to be done, before he let that threatening darkness close about him. There was she—the beloved—still to think of. He had to get her from that room, get her back to safety.

Swaying, he went across the room, sank beside her, gathered her limp, little body into his arms. For a moment wildly throbbing pulses beat together. But, again, with a fierce effort he commanded himself, recovered, lifted her, and struggled again to his feet.

Then came the torture of that awful descent by the spiral stairway. Every step he took was agony to him.

The wound in his shoulder was bleeding afresh and blood from the knife-cut in his hip reached to the top of his riding-boot.

Even when the foot of the spiral stairway had been reached, there was still an awful downward journey. It bewildered, tortured him.

But he would not give in! There was the possibility that some lurking Turk would come upon them—find him and the girl he carried—and he could not fight again.

Passing through a curtained entrance, he came at last out upon the balcony which half-encircled the hall of the palace.

Drawing a half-sobbing breath of relief, he tightened his hold of the girl, felt her soft breast all warm and throbbing against his.

Down in the hall stood the white men.

The Englishmen who had forced their way

into the Turkish palace were—Colonel Wayne and Lieutenant Marsh, Captain Price, Lieutenant Stuart, and Colonel Royston, who had come indirectly from Damascus with some of his men.

Having gained command in the hall, the English had swiftly released Conquest and, when he was recovered, had set about finding the white girl.

It happened that when Conquest, carrying the girl, had stepped onto the balcony, most of the Englishmen, including Wayne, Hadley, and Marsh, were in the hall, having just come from a fruitless search.

The Turk's son was also present, standing by the big couch in the centre with three chief natives.

A sudden silence fell upon the Englishmen as they saw the lovers upon the balcony. Then, when they would have spoken, something seemed to check their speech.

In the slim, wounded figure of the man carrying the lovely, half-clad body of the girl there was something arresting—almost awe-inspiring.

When he had reached the foot of the stairs, Colonel Royston took a step forward.

"Boy!—Julian—"

Colonel Wayne started forward from the other men.

"My child!—"

The arms of the man who carried her tightened a little more round the girl's slight body, as if he would hold her even from her father.

"She is—safe."

Wayne stood motionless.

"The Turk—?" began Price.

"He is—dead," said Julian Conquest in the same slow, forced tone.

The Turk's son spoke.

"You killed him—my father?"

"No—I did not kill him," returned Conquest. "I—would have done so—but he fell from the balcony of the room to which he'd taken the woman."

"Daphnne!" murmured the father.

"She is—unharmed," said Conquest. "She is—safe."

Bending, he laid the limp, lovely form of the girl upon the couch. Then, slowly, with difficulty, he drew himself to his feet. With quick words Colonel Wayne dropped to his knees beside the couch.

Colonel Royston sprang forward and caught Julian Conquest in his arms as the latter fell.

* * *

About a fortnight after the momentous day which saw the death of the Turk, the Englishmen were seated together in the Room of Mirrors.

Beyond the long terrace was a fair aspect of sunlit gardens and village. In the palace itself was a serene, languorous quietness, as though the awful disturbance of that day a fortnight past had never been.

On a couch in the centre, Julian Conquest half-sat, half-lay, with one arm in a tight sling.

"It was a mad thing to do, boy—mad!" exclaimed Colonel Royston, a tall, dark man, who sat on a small Eastern chair near the head of the couch. "What in Heaven's name possessed you?"

"Lord, it was a bit daring," added the young

Lieutenant Stuart. "It pretty nearly floored us all at the Consulate when we found out what you'd done."

"It was mad," repeated Colonel Royston. "Boy, what did you do such a thing for? You know what you are to me. If I'd have lost you, I'd have lost a son. When I heard what you'd done I came straight away from Damascus with some of my men—"

"Well, you see," Julian Conquest explained, "I got to know this Ahmad Hadi, the Turk's son. He thought I was a real Turk like himself and we got pretty friendly. I learnt a good deal about him. But he could tell me nothing of the Bey, since his father had sent him away to study and get some knowledge of the West when he was a boy.

"Then I heard that a car belonging to your party, Colonel Wayne, was found all smashed up near the Syrian, and the idea came to me to impersonate this son."

"It was a mad thing, Julian," commented Royston, but there was affection in his glance.

"But, Sir," laughter lightened the golden eyes, "it was the only way to get the Turk."

"Eh?"

"You know we had little chance of getting him as we were going on. He had to be fought in his own way. We had to play as daring and cunning a game as he."

"But you nearly lost," said Royston. "Indeed, it's pretty marvellous you got as far as you did without being found out."

"You certainly came—just in time," Julian Conquest said slowly. "I hardly dared to expect you. You say you followed the Turk's son?"

"Yes. I was determined to go after you and make an end of this Turk. But as you know, we hadn't much knowledge as to where this place of his was. Then someone hit upon the idea of following the Bey's son. We found out you'd had him seized and shut up in some place in Trenedad.

"Anyway we set him free, listened to his eloquence, and then followed him. Then Colonel Wayne and young Marsh suddenly came upon us. You may be sure we came pretty quick on to the palace after that. But, good God, boy, if we hadn't come—"

"Sir, we will not think—if you hadn't come," said Julian Conquest.

A Turkish youth softly entered the Room of Mirrors. He informed the white men that Ahmad Hadi Bey awaited them within the hall.

Julian Conquest, who, despite many protests, had decided to be present at this interview with the man he had impersonated, was the last to move towards the entrance.

Colonel Wayne waited for him and they stood a moment, talking.

"Lieutenant Conquest, I owe you so much. My blind folly might have cost you your life—"

"Instead," Conquest interrupted, "it was the Turk who lost. And I won—what was worth risking life for!"

"I've hardly had a chance to thank you for all you've done."

Conquest raised his free hand.

"Colonel Wayne, there's something I wish to speak to you about. I want you to give me something. Something which is very precious. I want your daughter."

Colonel Wayne looked into the golden eyes of the young Lieutenant for whom he had felt an instinctive liking.

"Isn't she yours already?"

Conquest looked away to the terrace and his hazel eyes with their darker lashes were beautiful with their almost brooding look.

"Well, perhaps, but I'd like to know that you don't mind losing her—to me."

"Julian." Wayne pressed the other's shoulder. "I can't say how happy I am. I'll be proud as Royston to have you for a son—"

Arm in arm the two men went out to the hall.

In the hall stood the Turk's son, Ahmad Hadi.

"I am aware how my father did sin grievously against you. I cannot express, *effendi*, my sorrow at this deplorable affair," said the Turk's son. "I was not in with the schemes of my father; therefore I have a suggestion to make. It is that you allow me to keep possession of this, our palace and province."

There was quick talk among the Englishmen and some murmur of dissent.

The Turk's son, his handsome face perfectly serene, went on:

"I know how greatly you have suffered at the hands of my father—for that I grieve—yet I have suffered some little at your hands. You do know how I beset in the town of Trenedad and imprisoned there in a house by one I knew as Dara Samara but who was, in truth, Lieutenant Conquest."

Captain Price bent to speak into the ear of the Captain Hadley.

"The Turk's got us there. That's our weak

point. Conquest's put us into a devil of an awkward situation."

With the same calm demeanour Ahmad Hadi continued:

"You need have no fear that I shall not be your friend. He, whom I knew as Dara Samara, can tell you that I knew nothing of the life and schemes of the Bey, my father, before, and that I have no feelings of enmity towards the English."

With golden eyes that held a glint of amusement Julian Conquest looked towards the Turk's son.

"That's true. You knew little about the Bey at all."

The glances of the two young men, the one white, the other native, met, and there was no hostility in their looks.

For a few minutes the Englishmen talked together; then Colonel Royston turned again to the Turk's son.

"We've taken note of what you say, Hadi Bey, and your request seems reasonable. We will consider the matter."

Chapter Ten

From a certain white villa in Damascus came the music of an orchestra. The gay, swiftly played dance-tunes sounded a little strange in the still, fragrant Eastern night.

In the villa, men and women stood or sat about, talking and laughing.

In the midst of one of these laughing, chattering groups stood Colonel Wayne and his daughter.

An evening-dress of soft white with sequins agleam on breast and on shoulder-bands clothed her small slender form, and the short fair curls were brushed back so that, beneath the lights, her head had the sheen of gold.

Looking about the room, Daphnne noted the gay, brilliant scene. It was one of so many that she had been in. This was her world—her old life.

Yet, in some strange way, it seemed to have altered. It was not the same. It was different.

After a while she escaped from the many friends in the villa, slipped out to the silent garden; from the blaze of electric-light to the pale radiance of the moon.

A moment she stood in the moonlight, breathing in the sweet, heavy perfume of the garden.

Turning her head, she looked across the garden. Before her lay Damascus, a city of dreams, silver-pale in moonlight, dusky in velvet shadow.

Slowly she moved, went forward through the scented dusk. Crossing a small courtyard before the villa, she stepped up to a terrace which overlooked the road.

He was there, leaning a little against the white parapet. The bright moonlight showed each to the other for one moment; the next she was in his arms and his lips were on hers.

Slowly the clinging strength of that sweet, close embrace relaxed. She drew out of his arms and he held her before him with slender hands clasping her bare shoulders.

"Daphnne! But why are you here? I thought this affair"—Conquest looked towards the villa—"was especially for you."

Daphnne, laughing a little, flushing in the darkness, took refuge in reproving him.

"Julian, Colonel Royston arranged a party at his place tonight in your honour! And you've deserted them!"

They looked at each other—and then laughed together, the happy, exultant laughter of lovers.

Then he had her close against him.

"Darling, I've longed for you so much. Nearly losing you in that palace told me how much I wanted you. I can hardly believe we won though. That I have you—all safe—my own!"

"But we did win!" She drew back a little from him, to look up at him with shining eyes.

"Yes, we won."

His golden eyes gleamed a little in the moonlight. On his dark young face there was now no trace of hardness—no arrogance in the hazel eyes, no cynical curl to the even lips.

Her hands rested on his arms, then moved slowly up to his shoulders.

"Did you doubt that we should, when you fought so well? Oh, Julian, how you fought in that palace!"

He moved his head with a sudden gesture and his golden eyes flashed a little. He laughed and she heard the underlying note of fierceness in that laughter.

"I felt wild enough. Oh, darling, do you realise how savage I was? I—I was quite surprised at myself—afterwards."

"You were wonderful!"

"Dearest you don't know the savageness that enters a man when the woman he loves is in danger. We can fight like beasts of the wild—fight with murder in our hearts—with no thought for anything but the safety of the beloved."

"Dear," her hand slipped through his dark hair with a touch that caressed, "our glory is in a love like that—"

"Daphnne," he had her swiftly in his arms, again close to him, her soft, light-clad body resting upon his strong, supple form, "when will you marry me? Dear, we've won through now; we've won our love; tell me when it shall be—?"

But she would not look at him then; laughing, panting, she struggled, slipped from his hold.

"Julian! I . . . I can't say all at once . . ."

He gazed at her fair, warm, half-averted face with steady, brilliant eyes, and smiled.

"Can I give Colonel Royston no reason for not sending me off again—"

She turned then, clung to him, soft, bare arms about him.

"Julian! You're not going to do any more work . . . take any more risk . . . ?"

He looked into her wide, dark eyes and laughed—happy, triumphant laughter—and with suddenly warm cheeks she hid her face against him.

"Oh, Julian," she tried to laugh a little herself then, "why have you made me love you so?"

"Dearest," he let the loosened gold curls rest against his lips, "do you think I'd let Colonel Royston or anyone send me from you now?"

She lay back in his arms.

"Do you think I can wait any longer, Daphnne?" He bent over her. "You're mine now—and I want you. If you won't say when you'll marry me—"

"Yes?"

"If you won't say when," his eyes gazed into hers with a look of the old mastery, "I'll act the Turk in real earnest again and carry you off—willing or unwilling!"

"Julian . . . I don't think I should even . . . struggle!"

"Daphnne!" He crushed her against him.

"Darling, you must tell me—when you'll be mine! Oh, my sweet, I can't wait! I've wanted you —for so long. I nearly lost you—and that makes me want you so much—so quickly—"

"Yes?" With half-closed eyes, half-smiling lips, she looked up at him.

"You've been mine, beloved, yet I've had to give you up! Had to let you go from me. Even when that gold head rested on my pillow—you were not mine. Even when you slept in my arms— you slept from fear—not love! Daphnne—"

She moved a little in his arms, faced him, a slim, fair figure utterly sweet and desirable in her surrender.

"Julian, why do you ask? Aren't I yours ... to do with as you like? My love," her small hands went up to his shoulders, "do you think I don't want to be yours ... quickly too? Do you think I don't want you? Julian, you know what my answer is!"

Her glance lingered on him, on this one man who was so dear, whose love could give her such glorious pleasure and happiness—

He looked down at her who was now his, experiencing the wild thrill of possession.

Her lips parted with a quick-drawn breath; her eyes closed from his brilliant look. He bent, his mouth closed upon her half-parted lips.

The scent of jasmine, rising upon the night air, filled the garden.

ABOUT THE EDITOR

BARBARA CARTLAND, the world's most famous romantic novelist, who is also an historian, playwright, lecturer, political speaker and television personality, has now written over 200 books.

She has also had many historical works published and has written four autobiographies as well as the biographies of her mother and that of her brother, Ronald Cartland, who was the first Member of Parliament to be killed in the last war. This book has a preface by Sir Winston Churchill.

Barbara Cartland has sold 100 million books over the world, more than half of these in the U.S.A. She broke the world record in 1975 by writing twenty books, and her own record in 1976 with twenty-one. In addition, her album of love songs has just been published, sung with the Royal Philharmonic Orchestra.

In private life, Barbara Cartland, who is a Dame of the Order of St. John of Jerusalem, has fought for better conditions and salaries for Midwives and Nurses. As President of the Royal College of Midwives (Hertfordshire Branch), she has been invested with the first Badge of Office ever given in Great Britain which was subscribed to by the Midwives themselves. She has also championed the cause for old people and founded the first Romany Gypsy Camp in the world.

Barbara Cartland is deeply interested in Vitamin Therapy and is President of the British National Association for Health.

Barbara Cartland

The world's bestselling author of romantic fiction. Her stories are always captivating tales of intrigue, adventure and love.

☐	13570	THE POWER AND THE PRINCE	$1.50
☐	13556	LOVE IN THE CLOUDS	$1.50
☐	11882	MAGIC OR MIRAGE	$1.50
☐	12841	THE DUKE AND THE PREACHER'S DAUGHTER	$1.50
☐	12569	THE GHOST WHO FELL IN LOVE	$1.50
☐	13035	LOVE CLIMBS IN	$1.50
☐	13036	A NIGHTINGALE SANG	$1.50
☐	13126	TERROR IN THE SUN	$1.50
☐	13392	ONLY LOVE	$1.50
☐	13446	WOMEN HAVE HEARTS	$1.50

Buy them at your local bookstore or use this handy coupon: